PATTERN OF MURDER

For cinema projectionist Sid Elbridge, it seems that things can't get any worse. First, circumstantial evidence has made him a police suspect in their investigation into a robbery at the cinema where he works. Next, his fiancée Vera is horribly killed in the same cinema, the victim of a falling light fixture. When Sid accidentally finds strange, intricate patterns traced in the dust on the wooden frame of a still case, his curious discovery will reveal a ruthless murderer . . .

JOHN RUSSELL FEARN

PATTERN OF MURDER

Complete and Unabridged

LINFORD
Leicester

First published in Great Britain

First Linford Edition
published 2009

British Library CIP Data

Fearn, John Russell, *1908 - 1960*.
    Pattern of murder- -(Linford mystery library)
    1. Motion picture projectionists- -Fiction.
    2. Evidence, Circumstantial- -Fiction.
    3. Detective and mystery stories.
    4. Large type books.
    I. Title II. Series
    823.9'12–dc22

    ISBN 978–1–84782–870–5

Published by
F. A. Thorpe (Publishing)
Anstey, Leicestershire

Set by Words & Graphics Ltd.
Anstey, Leicestershire
Printed and bound in Great Britain by
T. J. International Ltd., Padstow, Cornwall

This book is printed on acid-free paper

1

Bad day at the races

It was Tuesday afternoon at the Bartonwick Racecourse. For a brief time Vera Holdsworth was released from the dark abyss of the Cosy Cinema in the town's main street, where she worked as a head usherette.

'I have the feeling,' said the young man accompanying her, 'that I'm going to be lucky today. Not beginner's luck, either! Just to counter any wrong impressions you may have got, I might as well tell you that I've other interests besides running those blasted films in the Cosy Cinema.'

Vera glanced at him quickly. The statement had come as something of a surprise to her. She had always thought of Terry Lomond as a quiet worker with few ambitions outside of his job as chief projectionist.

'You mean you bet a lot, Terry?' she asked.

'Of course I do! I'm not the kind of dope who sits around waiting for pennies from heaven. Since, however, I'm nailed down in the projection room most of my life I do my betting over the 'phone.'

'So that's how you make your money! I've often noticed that you don't seem to be very short.'

Terry Lomond smiled.

'When do you start betting — or whatever it is?' Vera asked, as with Terry she made her way through the moving crowds and the late August sunshine.

'Soon. Keep going.'

'All right. Give me a cig, will you? I'm dying for one.'

Terry complied and the girl inhaled deeply after he had lighted it for her. Then she went on again. She did not argue about his directions. He had a determined way with him. Though he was invariably genial, it was somehow superficial: it never seemed to truly mirror the man. Certainly, Terry's face was not that of a genuinely cordial person. It was cast in a strong, cynical mould, with sharply defined mouth and jaw. The long nose

2

and grey-blue eyes lent him qualities that made him quite handsome. The worst feature was his hair — black and unruly, sticking out in bangs and tufts. It was the penalty for working most of his life in the midst of electrical static.

With Vera Holdsworth, Nature had been even less generous. What attractiveness she possessed lay in the subtle grace of her figure, becomingly revealed in the summer frock she was wearing. Otherwise, she was plain ordinary. Her nose was short, her chin self-indulgent — yet her clear blue eyes and carefully applied makeup did a great deal to balance Nature's omissions . . . Vera was the kind of girl who, given a decent chance, might have amounted to something. As it was, her virtues — which she only used when it suited her — were constantly overshadowed by her background. Her home life had never contributed anything towards developing the better side of her character.

'Just why haven't we been here before and had fun?' Vera looked about her interestedly. 'That's what I want to know.

You've been holding out on me, Terry!'

He looked at her with cynical amusement. 'Do it well, don't you?' he asked.

'Do it well? What in the world do you mean?'

'Why not be yourself?' Terry suggested. 'You don't have to come the nice little girl stuff with me, you know. I'm no angel. If I were I wouldn't want you for a companion . . . And it cuts both ways,' he added. 'You wouldn't have picked *me* for a boy friend had you thought me a saint.'

'Well, I . . . ' Vera hesitated and fumbled in her mind. 'I'm no prude, if that's what you mean. Not like Helen Prescott, for instance, with her frightfully honourable ideas.'

Terry was silent. A grim look had crossed his handsome face for a moment, then it faded just as quickly. He had a profound inner liking for Helen Prescott, another of the Cosy Cinema's usherettes — but somehow that pretty young lady always seemed to keep him at arm's length ever since she had started work at the cinema in 1952. Even now, five years later, his charm had still completely failed to impress her. And the cinema staff knew it, even to the extent of making sarcastic comment. Terry knew she had no other knowledge of him except that he was a quiet, steady worker, respectful to his employer and always a gentleman as far as the opposite sex was concerned.

'We'll leave Helen out of this,' Terry said presently, thinking.

Vera plumed smoke through her nostrils. 'All right with me, I'm sure. I've no time for her anyway, particularly as I seem to understand you a good deal better than she does.'

'Which is why you fixed your day off to coincide with mine?' Terry questioned dryly.

'Well — er — ' Vera hesitated. 'Could be.'

Again Terry was silent. He was finding it quite agreeable to discover, after all the rebuffs he had received from Helen Prescott, that at least one girl had gone out of her way to seek his company. Not that he had any real regard for Vera Holdsworth, but at least she was attractively female and therefore better than

5

nothing at all. Since he would have the task of settling down one day he might as well get started.

'I wish I had a fur coat,' Vera said unexpectedly — and Terry gave her a startled glance.

'What! On a day like this? It must be nearly eighty — '

'Not for today: I'm thinking about the winter. I get the most frightful colds leaving that hot cinema and charging out into the frost. One day it'll be pneumonia. Besides,' Vera added wistfully, 'I *am* the head usherette, after all.'

Terry seemed about to comment, and then he stopped. Vera looked surprised for a moment, than she understood the reason as the voices of two men, walking by, drifted clearly.

' . . . not a chance of it losing, Bob. Got it from the owner himself. 'Pirate's Cutlass!' '

'Three thirty, did you say?'

'Put your shirt on it. Forty to one, and . . . '

Terry looked at the girl. She raised an eyebrow and said nothing.

'Would that be manna from heaven?' Terry asked finally.

'I don't know about heaven: more like the horse's mouth!'

'It's started something, anyway . . . Let's see . . . ' Terry studied his race card and then moved across to the bookies' stands. He came back presently to where the girl was standing. 'Forty to one,' he confirmed. 'Rank outsider.'

He stood biting his lip and considering the dust, trying to make up his mind.

'I've got a quid I might risk,' Vera said, thinking — then she became aware of Terry's scornful glance.

'Never mind your quid! I'm going to play this hunch. I often do that and keep my fingers crossed. That chap did say to put your shirt on it. Here — take a look!'

Terry fumbled inside his hip pocket and brought out his wallet. The girl stared blankly at the bulge inside it. It was stuffed with treasury notes.

'For the love of Mike, Terry, how much money have you there?'

'Not so loud!' Terry cautioned, glancing about him. 'There are all kinds of wide boys around . . . There are two hundred pounds,' he told her. 'I've made it buying and selling sub-standard movie equipment. It's quite a racket with some projectionists. You want a fur coat, and there's a special projector I'm itching to buy. If I put this lot on the nag's nose and it comes off we'll both be satisfied — and have a lot to spare.'

'Yes, but . . . It's an awful lot of money.'

'I'm going to risk it, anyway. Now, where's the 'phone?'

''Phone?' Vera repeated. 'What about these bookies?'

'Not for me, sweetheart. I've got my own bookie, as I told you. I don't have to pay him on the nail since I run an account. With these blokes I'd have to pay on the spot. As long as I have cover for my bet I'm safe. Right! Two hundred to win on 'Pirate's Cutlass'. Come with me.'

He grabbed Vera's arm and hurried through the crowd. Within five minutes he had made his 'phone call to his own bookmaker. He came out of the telephone kiosk with a satisfied grin.

'Well, it's all done!' he announced.

'Now let's see what happens. The race is due after the next one.'

Vera walked beside him slowly, lighting another cigarette as she went.

'You've taken a frightful chance, Terry,' she said. 'If it doesn't come off you'll — '

'That's *my* worry, isn't it? Life's not worth living without taking a risk!'

The girl looked at him quickly, then away again.

'In a way,' he said, as they moved through the throngs, 'I suppose we sort of became engaged today. Funny, really! I never knew you felt that way about me — and to think I've wasted all that time on Helen and never been given any encouragement. You must have some sort of regard for me or you wouldn't have altered your day off to fit in with mine. If I've seemed a bit — well, distant, it was only because I didn't realize how things stood between us.'

Vera did not say anything until they reached a position where they could clearly see the course. Then she made a remark in a low voice.

'Don't take too much for granted, Terry.'

'Eh?' Quick surprise was in his eyes. 'Oh, you mean about the race? Oh, you don't have to worry. It's in the bag.'

'I'm not talking about the race: I'm talking about *us*. I don't really feel that way about you. I just enjoy your company, that's all. As usual, you're trying to make the grade single handed without giving anybody else a chance to speak.'

'You mean . . . ' Terry stopped and gave the girl a hard, searching look — but before he could say anything further the 3:30 had commenced and his attention, along with Vera's, was centred exclusively on the track.

In tense silence they watched the race begin: then their excitement got the better of them and they started yelling at the top of their voices and beating the rail in front of them. But gradually the tempo of their eagerness slowed down, and it seemed to Terry that the bottom dropped out of the world when 'Pirate's Cutlass' finished second by a short head.

'That,' Vera muttered, looking under her eyes, 'is that . . . ' She flirted her cigarette end over the rail. 'Maybe the nag was half starved, or something. Or the tipster could have been a liar.'

For several moments Terry did not speak. He stood and stared at the track, then as the girl nudged him he came back to awareness.

'We'd better be moving, hadn't we?' she asked. 'Or are you going to stare at the track all day?'

Terry still said nothing, but as the girl shrugged and moved on he turned to follow her. In time they came to the grass banks near the gates. Terry sat down and gazed in front of him. Vera coiled up beside him and waited. The silence positively hurt.

'Was I nuts, or what?' Terry demanded suddenly, thumping his forehead. 'Two hundred quid to win — all gone with the wind! Why in hell didn't I back it for a place as well?'

'You laid the bet,' Vera sighed. 'I didn't even hear what you said to the bookie. Don't even know who he is, or anything about him. It's all your doing.'

Terry gave her a look of disgust and

then lay on his side with his back to her. He chewed a wisp of grass for several minutes. Then he sat up and said loudly,

'I wouldn't have bet at all if it hadn't been for your damned fur coat!'

Vera opened her mouth in blank amazement. Then her blue eyes slitted.

'Hey now, just a minute! Don't start blaming me! What about that substandard projector you're itching to get? You intended to bet, for coat or otherwise, after you'd had that hot tip!'

Terry spat the grass out of his mouth and looked at Vera moodily. When he spoke he had changed the subject.

'Look, Vera, what did you mean about not 'feeling that way' about me?'

Vera took an enamalled case out of her handbag and lighted another cigarette. She lay back on her elbows and surveyed him, the smoke drifting into her eyes.

'I meant what I said, that's all. I can't help it if you jump to conclusions, can I?'

'I'm not taking that for an answer!' Terry's blue-grey eyes were bright and accusing. 'For the last eight weeks we've been out together every Tuesday — and *you* arranged it. You fixed your day off to coincide with mine. What conclusion am I supposed to draw from that except that you wanted to be with me?'

'I *did* want to be with you, but it doesn't have to go any further than that, does it? You take too much for granted, and always have!' Vera changed suddenly to the defensive. 'In our sort of job there isn't much opportunity to make friends outside the cinema staff. I don't want to spend my time with one of the girls who might be off on the same day I am. No darned fun in that. I *can't* spend the time with Sid because when you are away he has to be in charge of the box. So what else was there for it but for me to cotton on to you?'

'Sid?' Terry repeated, wondering. Sidney Elbridge was the second projectionist. 'What's he got to do with it? You don't mean that you and Sid are — ?'

'Not exactly. We're just friendly.'

'Then why don't you take Monday off when he does?'

'I tried to, but the boss wouldn't hear of it. He said it would leave us short staffed.'

How much truth there was in this Terry did not know. The loss of two hundred pounds had, for the moment, dulled his power to think straight.

'What it boils down to,' he said slowly, 'is that you're a cheap little two-timer! First you have me on a string, and then Sid. What are you out for? The best catch?'

Vera set her mouth and nipped the glowing end from her cigarette.

'What the hell sort of talk do you call that, Terry? *I* didn't make you lose your two hundred pounds, did I?'

'I think you did! All that talk about a fur coat started it. You tagged on to me because you noticed I don't seem to be short of money. You even admitted the fact! You've been thinking you could do better by hanging on to me instead of Sid, who's got nothing beyond his wages because he hasn't the brains to try and make money.'

Vera flared. 'Rot!'

Terry's right hand flashed up and struck hard across the girl's face. He just couldn't help himself. It made her head jerk. Her fingers quivered up to her cheek. Terry sat looking at her, feeling as though it had been another person who'd struck the blow.

'I'm . . . sorry,' he muttered.

Vera got to her feet without a word, picking up her handbag. She started walking away. Terry lay where he was, watching her go and thinking what a perfect figure she had. Then she became part of the crowd and was gone . . . Terry sighed and reflected. He was wondering now if he regretted thc thing he had done. It had been impulse — hot tempered impulse.

'Sucker,' he muttered finally. 'Sucker! That's what you are! Anyway, Vera's pretty low class. I wouldn't have bothered with her at all if Helen hadn't given me the air. Wonder *why* Helen doesn't give me a break? I don't look so bad, and my intentions are straight . . . '

His thoughts clouded. Perhaps — the manager? Mark Turner, the owner-manager of the Cosy Cinema, was only thirty-two years of age, quiet mannered and worth a good deal of money by inheritance. He seemed to have a profound interest in Helen's welfare.

'That's it,' Terry growled. 'She's out for bigger fish. I can't blame her, I suppose — Anyway, what I've got to do is hand over two hundred of the best for this day's work, and the sooner the better. George Naylor doesn't like to be kept waiting.'

Gloomily, he thrust his hand inside his hip pocket. Almost immediately he became rigid and felt his scalp crawling. There was only the flatness of his pocket and no sign of the bulging wallet. He jumped to his feet and began a frantic searching through his suit. The answer remained the same. The wallet had gone.

In his desperation his thoughts flashed to Vera. Had she taken it? He shook his head stubbornly. No; she might be a two-face, but there was no reason to suppose she was a thief. Still, she *had* wanted a fur coat — No! Terry set his jaw. There was only one right answer. He must have flashed the notes more ostentatiously than he had intended and some light fingered gentleman had relieved him of the lot, including wallet . . . His money, union card, odds and ends of all sorts, had gone.

Now what? In a little cul-de-sac off the high street George Naylor was expecting £200. When paid on the nail he was genial enough. He even smiled when he paid out. He would *not* smile when he saw £200 was likely to be owing indefinitely.

'Hell!' Terry muttered. 'I've as much chance of getting two hundred in a hurry as flying to the moon!'

Various lines of action weaved through his mind. He thought first of Mark Turner. He was a friendly soul and he might advance £200, but he would want to know for why. He would not approve of his chief projectionist gambling to the extent of £200 a time. It would be tantamount to asking for the sack. Besides, Turner was away this week on a trade-show routine. No chance of contacting him. Terry himself was deputy-manager for the time being.

Terry's speculations switched to Dick

17

Whiteley, the second-hand dealer in sub-standard movie equipment with whom he did a good share of business. That gaunt-faced, tight-lipped gentleman would not be likely to advance a penny, unless somehow the heat could be turned on him.

Moneylenders?

'No!' Terry said flatly. 'Only one thing for it. Have to make a clean breast of it to Naylor, and see what he says.'

His mind made up he left the racecourse as quickly as possible and a 'bus took him into the town — the small but thriving town of Bartonwick. Half a mile down the main street Terry alighted and hurried off down a side road. Here was a huddle of houses and three shops. Two of the shops dealt in antiques and the third in needlework. At the far end of the cul-de-sac was a Dickensian-looking house transformed into a far more commercial purpose. A brass plate said:

George Naylor — Turf Accountant.

Terry entered the front door of the house-cum-office, went through the short

18

hall, and into the back room. George Naylor was sprawled in the swivel chair at his littered desk. He was big, and fat, and sweaty black hair lay plastered on his round head to conceal the bald spots. He peered up at Terry through fleshy bags of eyes.

'Hello, Terry. That's what I like to see — a prompt payer. Looks as if you took a caning with 'Pirate's Cutlass,' too. Short head! Too bad!'

'Yes, a short head,' Terry agreed. 'Which means I owe you two hundred.'

'According to my reckoning, yes.'

Silence. George Naylor lighted a cigarette and blew out the match with an emphatic puff of breath.

'Matter of fact,' Terry said, 'I've come to ask a favour.'

George Naylor did not speak, or move. He lay like a mass of rubber in his swivel chair, waiting.

'I've been robbed,' Terry added. 'My wallet was pinched while I was at the racecourse.'

'Was it now?' George Naylor shrugged his heavy shoulders. 'You should be more careful, shouldn't you? I'm surprised at you, the fly boy!'

'I'm trying to tell you, George, that I can't pay up at the moment.'

Naylor knocked the ash from his cigarette and then leaned flabby forearms on the desk. He peered up at Terry intently.

'Look, Terry, business is business. I don't know what crackpot notion prompted you to put two hundred on that nag — and to win too! But when you come here without the two hundred to settle up you're playing with dynamite. Fact remains, I want the money! I'm not insisting on it right now: two hundred takes a bit of getting, I know. We'll have to come to some sort of arrangement. Instalments, eh?'

'Even that's going to be difficult.'

'I'm being as fair as I can afford to be. I've my own interests to think of. If you can't stand the loss of two hundred quid you shouldn't have bet that much, that's all. That's commonsense.'

'I tell you it was a genuine bet! I *had* the money then. It was stolen from me afterwards.'

George Naylor heaved out of his chair

and drew hard at his cigarette.

'It's up to you, Terry. Instalments are the only way out. Let's say four instalments of fifty pounds each — and I'm being generous at that. Let's see now — today's Tuesday. I'll give you 'til a week next Saturday to get the first instalment. That's fair enough, isn't it? Sixteen whole days in which you can turn round.'

'And suppose I don't succeed?' Terry asked. 'I can plead the Gaming Act, you know, by which all contracts 'whether by parole or in writing, by way of gaming or wagering, shall be null and void'.'

'Gaming Act 1845, replaced by a tougher one in 1892.' Naylor gave a grim look. 'Don't try the Smart Alec routine with me, Terry!'

'You can't *make* me pay! That's the main point!'

'I can make you smart, though, and by God I will if it becomes necessary. And I don't think you'd publicly declare anything about being mixed up with the Gaming Act, either. If I don't get that money I'll do other things.'

'Such as?' Terry demanded.

21

'Well, for one thing you have a manager who'd cut your throat if he knew you'd been gambling — which is one reason why I don't think you'll plead the Gaming Act. I *know* Turner: he doesn't even like me as a paying patron because he knows I'm a bookie . . . One gentle, well-placed hint would rock the boat for you nicely, Terry, wouldn't it? It's so easy to prevent, too. Just get the instalments, and we'll remain good friends.'

Terry did not say any more. He turned and left the office, mooching up the cul-de-sac to the main road once more . . .

* * *

When Terry arrived at the Cosy Cinema at quarter to nine the following morning he was in a black mood. Nor was it lightened any by the greeting of the doorman, busy in the wide foyer with the long, snaking tube of the vacuum cleaner.

'By heck, Terry, Sid hasn't 'arf got it in for you! Some time since I've seen him so riled.'

22

Terry came to a stop and frowned. 'Sid has? What the blazes is the matter with *him*, anyway?'

'I'm not quite sure, but he's in a rare tear. Seems to think the time's come to smear you on the walls!'

'Oh, he does, does he?' Terry smiled bitterly. 'For a second to set about his chief is nearly as bad as striking a superior officer . . . Where is he at the moment?'

The doorman looked about him and then seemed to remember. He snapped his fingers.

'Last I saw of him he was in the stalls, larking about with the girls. Not that I blame 'im for that. I like a bit of fun myself sometimes. Helps to cheer up this lousy 'ole we 'ave to work in.'

Larking with the girls was not a pastime of which Terry approved — not from any personal distaste but because his position as chief projectionist made it essential for him to keep his own particular staff in order, or explain to the manager. He murmured something inaudible to the doorman and then finished his walk across the wide foyer and pushed aside the glass doors to enter the cinema's lower floor. It was wide and barren and smelled of stale tobacco smoke. There was only one naked 750-watt lamp high in the ceiling, casting its pallid light on chair backs and the scarf-wrapped heads of the usherettes as they moved about and dusted.

Terry paused by the back row, gazing over the expanse. His eye caught Vera Holdsworth's as she rose from cleaning a seat. She gave him an icy stare.

'Where's Sid?' Terry demanded suddenly.

Low down on the right hand side of the proscenium a figure appeared in a doorway. He had a mop and empty bucket in his hands. Not that there was anything unusual about this. All the cleaning tackle was kept in the storeroom back stage, where once an orchestra pit had been.

'I'm coming,' Sid Elbridge called, in a surly voice. 'Give me a chance, can't you?'

He moved up the right-hand gangway deliberately. He was big, ungainly, with sandy hair and turned-up nose. His main virtue was that he was a clever electrician and could be relied on to run a show by himself in a crisis. The only thing he did not like was having to work in the evenings. He was twenty-five, five years younger than Terry.

'What's all this rot about wanting to smear the wall with me?' Terry snapped, as Sid came up. 'Harry's full of it. I've just been talking to him.'

'And Harry's right.' With a clatter Sid tossed down the bucket and flung the mop into it. 'I want a word with you, Terry — and right here is as good a place as any.'

Terry glanced about him. Heads had popped up behind seat backs in various directions, each head with a coloured duster or scarf wound round it.

'This is going to be good,' commented Kathleen Gatty, who liked nothing better than a quarrel, providing she was not mixed up in it.

'What's the matter, Sid?' called Helen Prescott. 'What are you getting so tough about?'

25

'That's what *I'm* wondering,' Terry said, and to Sid he added, 'If you've something on your mind let's go up to the box and talk it over — '

'To blazes with the box! We'll do it right here, Terry. I want to know what you mean by slapping Vera across the face as you did.'

Terry did not answer immediately. He could smell danger. Sid Elbridge was a slow mover as a rule, but when he did get excited he did it properly. Just at this moment he was obviously having a hard struggle to remain calm.

'I shouldn't try and deny it, Terry, if I were you.' Vera came up the gangway, tossing a duster from one hand to the other. 'You didn't think I was going to take a wallop like that without telling everybody what a rotten beast you are, did you?'

'How much else did you tell 'em?' Terry demanded.

'How much would you *like* me to tell 'em? I've simply made it clear that you're a low down heel — '

'Vera means a lot to me, Terry,' Sid cut

in, curtly. 'I want an apology for what you did to her yesterday, and if I don't get it I'll beat you up. You know I can do it, too.'

Terry did know it. Sid was nearly six feet tall and massively built.

'Do that, and you'll get yourself fired,' Terry replied, his voice brittle. 'Or have you forgotten that I'm the deputy manager while the boss is away? Lay a finger on me and out you'll go — on your ear! I'll see to that!'

'I'll risk it.' Sid clenched his big fists. 'And what's more, I think it was a dirty rotten trick to go behind my back on your day off and take Vera to the races. What right had *you* to go out with her? She's *my* girl, and I'm the only one she'll walk out with — when we get the chance.'

'I didn't know she was smitten with you until she told me,' Terry responded coldly.

'You ought to be damned well ashamed of yourself!' Sid went on. 'Betting two hundred pounds on a horse and then losing it! Why, most of us here — in fact probably *all* of us — hasn't even smelled that much money. I know I haven't. It makes me sore. Here am I, scrimping and scraping to get enough money to put down a deposit on a house, for Vera and me to live in when we get married, and then you chuck it about all roads!'

'What I do with my own money is no concern of yours! And I might add that you've kept your attachment to Vera mighty dark, haven't you?'

'Why not? You don't think either of us is going to broadcast our private affairs, do you? I wouldn't be raising this rumpus now except for the way you've been carrying on, Terry.'

Terry's eyes strayed to Helen Prescott. She was watching intently from side-stalls. Naturally she had heard every word and by this time must be thinking many things. Knowing only one side of the argument it could only look to her as if Vera had been slapped in the face for no good reason.

'I'm sorry I hit you, Vera,' Terry said at last, but he did not look at her as he spoke. 'I said so at the time. I lost my temper.'

'I'll say you did!' Vera retorted. 'And two hundred quid as well! You ought to be — '

'I've said I'm sorry, haven't I? Let it go at that!'

Terry swung away, his set face reflecting the bitterness of his emotions.

2

Robbery

Leaving the stalls, Terry went up the broad, white-rubbered staircase where the cleaning women were busy with buckets, rags, and disinfectants. To their greetings he made no response as they glanced significantly at one another. In a moment or two he had reached the half-turn on the staircase. Here was a polished doorway marked *Strictly Private*. He opened it, went beyond, and closed it.

He had passed now from the superficial comfort of the cinema into his own little world. Brick walls, defaced with NO SMOKING signs. White, concrete steps rising upwards to twenty feet. Cold air from wide ventilation slats, and a gradually deepening smell of amyl-acetate and half dissipated carbon fumes. At the top of the stone steps he turned sharp left and entered the low-ceilinged winding room. He stood thinking.

'Morning, Terry,' greeted the youth at the winding bench, looking up from inspecting the splice in the film he had just repaired. 'Not looking too pleased with yourself. Anything up?'

'Get on with your job and stop asking questions.'

'Okay, okay! You don't have to get tough about it.'

Billy Trent grandiloquently called himself 'the third projectionist'. To the staff and trade he was simply a re-wind boy. Just sixteen, he had untidy fair hair and the kind of blue eyes and delicate complexion that any girl would have been proud to possess.

Moodily, Terry departed for the projection room overhead, and presently Sid arrived and began to get busy with the mop. Terry glanced at him, then gazed absently through the porthole of Machine No. 1 into the great, pale-lit void of the cinema ... No sense in keeping up the squabble, he told himself. He, Sid, and Billy were compelled to live their working lives on top of one another.

'I'm sorry, Sid.' Terry turned finally and shrugged. 'I'm just that way out this morning. You see, as far as Vera's concerned, I thought she meant everything she said. I honestly got the shock of my life when I found she's as good as engaged to you. You might have let me have some hint.'

Sid relaxed. Normally good-natured, he took instant advantage of the break in the storm clouds.

'I couldn't do that, Terry. We're not officially engaged. I haven't the cash yet to buy a ring — but we certainly mean a lot to each other. You can't blame me for demanding an explanation when she said you'd hit her across the face.'

'No, I suppose not,' Terry admitted. 'There's something I can't understand, though. What do you see in the girl?'

'You saw enough in her to go out with her, didn't you? In fact you've been out with her quite a lot of times. She told me so.'

'Yes, but . . . ' Terry mused. 'Funny thing, but I never really got to know her until yesterday. I'd always thought of

32

her as a pretty decent girl, though on the lookout for number one just the same. Then yesterday I sort of saw her for the first time. What few virtues she has — and they *are* few — all seemed to vanish. It was quite a surprise to me.'

'Vera,' Sid said doggedly, 'is one of the best! The trouble is that she's had a poor upbringing, and her home life is nothing to shout about. She's all right if you understand her — as I do. I've made it my business to.'

Terry was silent for a moment, and then he shrugged.

'All right, let's forget all about it. You can be sure I shan't bother to go out with her again . . . I know I'd better hop down to the boss's office and see what's doing. I'd almost forgotten for the moment that I'm his deputy.'

The owner-manager's office was at the base of the Circle staircase, marked by a shiny door inscribed *Private*. Terry pulled out the duplicate key that Turner had given him and turned it in the lock. In the office, bright morning sunlight streamed through a window barred on the outside.

33

Burglaries had led the owner-manager to adopt this precaution.

Terry sat down in the swivel chair and pondered. Two hundred pounds! The fracas with Sid had been as nothing compared to this major worry. Absently Terry's eyes moved to the massive safe by the window. It was an old safe, combination locked, and perched on a brick foundation. Terry pushed a hand slowly through his unruly hair.

'Come in,' he called, at a knock on the door.

Madge Tansley, the head cashier, entered. In one hand she had a steel cash box, and under her arm was a booking plan on a square of boarding. She was tall, dark, and unemotional.

'I want my booking-plan sheet for today,' she said.

Terry eyed her and then went to the cupboard where the booking plans were kept. He handed her a new one.

'I'll put this cash box in the safe whilst I'm here' she added. 'Must be about two hundred pounds in it. That last picture did extremely well.'

'Glad to hear it.' Terry said. 'Usually we take a beating these days, thanks to television . . . However, I can't open the safe. I don't know the combination.'

'But I do. Mr. Turner gave it to me before he went away.'

Terry did not answer. The mention of £200 had stirred his mind into action again. He watched as Madge Tansley took a slip of paper from her pocket, and afterwards he watched every detail. Five right, six left, two right, seven left. The lock clicked.

When Madge looked again Terry was examining a batch of stills for the next feature picture.

'That's that,' Madge Tansley said — and departed.

Terry looked at the inscriptions in the light dust on top of the desk. He had traced them with his finger . . . 5-R, 6-L 2-R, 7-L. He transferred the information to a slip of paper and put it in his pocket, then he wiped the dust with the sleeve of his coat.

Two hundred pounds! Enough to pay off Naylor in one sweep. He could lay his hands on it right now — but that would never do. Too bald — too blatant, and no chance of getting away with it. Careful thought was needed. He sank down in the swivel chair and lighted a cigarette absently. He had been smoking it for a few moments before he realized it was a Turkish one that Sid had given him. Sid had a curious liking for them.

Taking it out of his mouth, Terry made a wry face, stubbed the Turkish in the ashtray, then lighted one of his own brand. It occurred to him suddenly that to remain in the office when there was obviously nothing for him to do might look suspicious — so he left, locking the door.

Harry, the doorman, came in from the stalls as Terry emerged.

'Can I order some more coke, Terry, or do I have to wait for the boss's okay?'

'Order it,' Terry answered briefly.

He turned to the staircase. Helen Prescott was coming down it backwards, dusting the gilded balustrade supports as she came.

Terry went slowly down the stairs until

he was level with her.

'Hallo, Helen,' he said quietly.

She turned from her job of dusting to look at him. 'Oh, hello, Terry. Anything I can do?'

'Do? Not particularly. Why?'

'Well, since you're the deputy manager you can give orders.'

'Oh, forget that! If there's anything at all I do want, it is to explain something to you.'

Helen inspected her duster and then raised her eyes. 'It wouldn't be about Vera, would it? You hitting her?'

'You don't have to put it that way,' Terry protested.

'In that case,' Helen said, 'why should you want to explain it all over again? You did that pretty effectively earlier on, didn't you?'

'That's just the point; I did not. That wasn't the whole story by a long shot, Helen. I want you in particular to know that the whole thing was a ghastly mistake. I found that Vera had been leading me up the garden and it made me see red. I'd hit her before I knew it.'

'What about it?' Helen asked coolly. 'Why justify yourself to *me*?'

'Because . . . Because I really am concerned as to what you think about me. You've known for months that I'm fond of you. I've tried in every possible way to show you as much — what bit of time we've had to see each other. Why can't you break down and give me a bit of encouragement?'

'I just don't know,' Helen admitted frankly. 'Can't be because you're repulsive. You're not that.'

'Then why don't you give me a chance?' Terry insisted.

'Mmm, maybe I will,' Helen reflected. 'All right, I'll wait for you after the show tonight.'

'Do that!' Terry's face brightened. 'I'll be a bit late because it's film stripping night and the programme has to be put ready to go back. Always the same on Wednesday night with the half weekly change. Anyway, I shouldn't be more than ten minutes behind.'

''Struth, ain't love grand?' the doorman asked, as he prowled from stalls to foyer.

38

'Nice legs you've got, lass,' he added approvingly, peering up the staircase.

'Oh, go and shout your prices!' Helen called after him.

'You'd better take care he doesn't hit you as hard as be did me, Helen,' added another voice.

Helen and Terry looked across the foyer. Vera Holdsworth had been standing behind a fall-length cutout of Rock Hudson, as hc would appear in a forthcoming feature. Presumably Vera had been dusting the cutout. Certainly she must have heard everything.

'Depends if I *deserve* hitting, doesn't it?' Helen asked pointedly.

'I'll see you tonight,' Terry muttered.

He went on his way and then up the second flight of steps, which led to the Circle. He wanted the chance to think by himself, and this seemed as good a place as any. But he was not alone, after all. Against the left hand wall, perched on a ladder, was Sid. He was working on a high wooden structure in-banded as a still picture frame.

Ignoring him, Terry sat down on the

second seat of Row A.

'Two hundred pounds,' he muttered to himself. 'There's only one way in which that can vanish without implicating me, and that's by a faked burglary. We've been burgled twice before — the lavatory window each time. Can't use the office window now those bars are there. I've a passkey to the building, which makes the thing dead easy. Mmm . . . anyway, the boss can afford it and I've got to tip up to Naylor or I'll be in a spot — '

Violent hammering made him jump. Sid was at work. The still frame was one of the manager's ideas. For two reasons it had to be perched above the head of anybody passing it. Stills had a habit of vanishing if they were within reach, and the law demanded a certain head clearance. Electrical work was not Sid's only accomplishment. He was a passably good joiner, too . . .

★   ★   ★

Sid made a point of catching up with Vera Holdsworth when she left the cinema for lunch. She did not reveal any particular surprise as his fast running footsteps caught up with hers.

'Well, did I do it right?' he questioned.

'Oh you mean about Terry?' Vera glanced at his big, eager face. 'Yes, I suppose so, but I'd have liked something a bit more — er — persuasive. You know! A fellow who hits a girl across the face wants more than just a ticking off. I'll bet you're as thick with him now as you ever were.'

'Well — yes,' Sid admitted uncomfortably. 'But look, Vera, it isn't because I think any the less about you. You don't know how it is in the projection room. You're on top of each other and you've got to maintain a certain air of peace.'

They both walked on in silence for a while as Vera appeared to be thinking matters over. Then she said slowly,

'You think I'm vindictive, Sid, don't you?'

'No,' Sid answered simply. 'I can quite understand how you feel. If I were a girl and had suffered the same sort of insult I think I'd be every bit as sore. Just the same, I'd be much happier if you didn't

41

go out with Terry again.'

'You needn't worry. I won't — under any circumstances!'

Silence again. They had reached the road where the girl's home stood before Sid spoke again.

'Listen, Vera, you know how I feel about you,' he said seriously. 'Why can't we take a risk and get tied up? I mean — I'll try and get another job somewhere with better pay. As a chief. I'm experienced enough.'

Vera reflected. 'I don't like taking a risk of that sort, Sid. Not as far as marriage is concerned. There's no guarantee that you'd ever get a better job, and if you didn't what sort of pinching and scraping would we have to endure? Start trying to find something, by all means — then let's talk again. Safest, don't you think?'

'I suppose so,' Sid sighed. 'I feel now, more than ever, that we ought to get married, if only to protect you. Things would be different with me as your husband . . . And it's me you should have, you know,' he added urgently. 'I'm about the only one who really understands you.'

★ ★ ★

Terry was fairly cheerful during the matinee, and by the time the night performance began he was apparently his old, carefree self. Neither Sid nor Billy had any more complaints to register against him. They even found they could joke with him without him taking offence. What neither of them knew was that his cheerfulness was occasioned by the fact that his plan was complete. He knew how be was going to get the £200 from the safe. So simple, too . . .

Terry had just finished lacing up his machine with film. As a matter of habit he gazed through the porthole on to the Circle. It was filling rapidly.

'Pretty as a picture, isn't she?' Sid asked in admiration.

'Pretty?' Terry repeated, frowning. 'Who?'

'Vera, of course. Or shouldn't I bring up the subject?'

Terry did not answer. He could see Vera clearly enough. The auditorium was brightly lighted now with six three-hundred watt lamps, three on each side of the ceiling. Each lamp was inside a massive heavy opal globe fitting. Terry did not like those globes. They had tremendous weight. More than once he had had the uneasy fear that one of them might come down one day.

Down in the Circle, Vera was in charge of tickets, and she was not exerting herself either. She rarely did. Now she had become the head usherette — mainly because the preceding usherette had departed to get married — she seemed to think she could be as lazy as she wished. She merely indicated the seats to the patrons and left it at that. In the quiet spells she sat on the spring tip-up seat fixed to the panelling at the side of the staircase. From this position she could see people approaching up the second half of the stairs. The tip-up seat was there by law, conforming to the regulation that no usherette must stand above a certain length of time. But for the handrail, which came just about the middle of her back, Vera would no doubt have lolled comfortably. As it was she had to sit erect, whether she liked it or not.

'You can have her,' Terry said at length, shrugging.

Sid gave him a look and then walked into the tiny adjoining steel-lined room where lay the turntables and slide lantern. In a moment or two a Sousa march was rattling noisily from the monitor-speaker in the projection room ceiling. The reverberation of the bass notes in the cinema itself struck against the glass of the portholes and made it quiver slightly. Sound vibrations were always strongest at this point in the building, coming in a straight line from the huge speakers at the back of the screen.

Terry glanced at the electric clock in the cinema. It was 7-10. He lounged across to the sound equipment and examined it perfunctorily. Everything was in order for the show. The triple button marked 'Non-sync — Projector — Output' was in the correct first position. The second position was for film sound, and the third for microphone announcements made from the box over the public address system. It was not often used. The last time had been when Johnny

Brown had got lost and Turner had been asked to locate him in the cinema.

'Two hundred pounds . . . ' Terry's thoughts reverted to it as he mused. He smiled to himself.

For ten minutes longer he waited, then he walked down the projection room to an open doorway and went out on to the exterior grating platform where the fire escape began its final descent. It was a habit of his to check that the escape was always in order.

'Twenty-five past,' Sid sang out, changing a record.

Terry climbed back to the projection room again and concentrated his mind on the job. He pressed the switches that flooded the proscenium curtains with multicolour. The Circle was more or less full now.

As usual Vera Holdsworth was on the tip-up seat, her back against the handrail, her head lolling slightly forward and her face turned towards the curtains. In the lap of her uniform lay the gleaming length of her torch.

The fingers of the electric clock had

moved on to 7-30. Terry pressed the button that opened the curtains, turned the dimmer control, which brought the glow of the houselights down to extinction, and then started up his machine. The news began. At this moment he felt, as always, that he had just started a journey. The responsibility for perfection of presentation lay with him.

This evening his interest in his work kept wandering. He wanted the show over and done with, so that he could hurry on with his plan. Mechanically, he ran his machine and, without a hitch, the show finished at its scheduled time of 9-50.

Terry did not waste a moment. He had Helen to meet, and then a job to do. He only stayed in the projection room long enough to make sure the fireproof shutters were down, then he hurried into the winding room. Whistling piercingly, Billy had flung the last film can into its transit case and Sid was scrambling into his dirty old mackintosh.

'Okay?' Terry asked, putting on his suit jacket.

'Except for the apeman,' Billy replied.

Sid glared ferociously and then straddled a heavy transit case. He heaved it up on to his broad shoulder. All three went down the stone stairs one after the other and emerged into the wet, steamy humidity of the cinema proper.

'See you tomorrow, Terry,' Sid called back, from lower down the staircase.

'Fair enough, Sid. Good night.'

Terry deliberately lagged behind. He saw Sid plant the transit case near the front door, take the news-can from Billy, and then check up the transport logbook and put it down on the larger case. This done, Billy departed, just missing a well-aimed kick at his rear. Sid hung about until Vera came hurrying down the staircase from the staff room.

'What about tonight's cash, Terry?' Madge Tansley called. 'Shall I put it in the safe?'

'Er — ' Terry demurred, anxious to be on his way. 'How much is there?'

'About eighty-two pounds with advance bookings.'

'Lock it in your cash desk for tonight. I'm in a hurry.'

Madge nodded, did as ordered, and then departed.

'So ends our day,' murmured Helen Prescott, coming into view drawing on her gloves. 'Ready, Terry?'

'Sure thing. Let's go.'

They crossed the foyer. Terry switched off the lights and then the main switch. He held the front doors open for the girl to pass. He locked them securely on the outside and he and Helen went down the steps into the cool dark of the summer night. There were still quite a few people strolling about.

'Terry,' Helen said seriously, 'I wouldn't be playing fair if I didn't warn you that this isn't going to get us anywhere. You'd rather have me frank about it, wouldn't you?'

Terry glanced at her. 'I maintain that you can't be frank about it when you've never even talked to me for above five minutes at a time. We've known each other for years, but for some reason you've always gone out of your way to turn the power off just when we're getting warmed up. I don't see any earthly reason

49

why we can't make a go of it.'

'That's one trouble with you, Terry: you see things too much from your own viewpoint. Don't get sore at me for telling you, will you? I don't know whether you do it intentionally or whether you've never realized it. I don't think you do it with your own sex: certainly I've never heard the boys complain in that respect. But all the girls think you're too possessive.'

'And Vera Holdsworth in particular thinks so, I suppose?'

'*All* of them! It never seems to occur to you that us girls might have notions of our own. For instance — you can't see why you and I shouldn't make a go of it. Doesn't it occur to you that *I* might see why we can't?'

'Just can't be a reason,' Terry said calmly. 'I know all about you, and there's no apparently logical reason for you turning me down.'

Helen came to a stop as they reached the end of the road in which her home stood. She looked at him seriously in the glow of the street lamp.

50

'Honestly, Terry, you do take too much for granted. I'm glad to have had this chance to talk to you if only to try and show you that you're a bighead. I like you, and I think you're a good chap to work with, but because I believe in being honest about my emotions I'm telling you that we'll not get anywhere together.'

'I suppose,' Terry said slowly, 'that this is a polite way of telling me that there's another chap somewhere?'

Helen hesitated. 'Well, not necessarily.'

'What about the boss? Don't think I haven't noticed that you are his favourite usherette.'

Helen laughed shortly. 'You don't ever give a girl a fair chance, do you? Flare up at the slightest provocation! I'm not surprised that Vera got swiped for something you didn't quite like . . . Anyway, thanks for seeing me home. See you tomorrow.'

Terry tightened his lips, swung on his heel, and departed up the street. After a while he stopped under a lamp and checked his watch. He had half an hour to kill before he put his plan into action.

By then it would be completely dark. He began walking back down the high street, thinking as he went . . .

He continued wandering for thirty minutes and by this time had come back to the cinema again. A brief glance up and down the street satisfied him that it was deserted. Quickly he drew out his keys, opened the doors, and glided into the foyer. He locked the doors again behind him.

With complete familiarity he walked swiftly through the dark, warm expanse until he reached the manager's door. Here he again fumbled with his keys. By touch he selected the one he wanted. Next he tugged a pair of rubber gloves from his pocket — with which he normally did most of his electrical work — and snapped them on his hands.

Opening the door gently he glided into the office and went over to the cupboard where the spare torches were kept. He found one and switched it on. Masking the glow with his hand he left the office and sped swiftly up the Circle staircase to a lavatory. With a strong thrust of his hand he pushed the double-sashed window outwards. The single clamp across both frames gave way at the screws, just as he had expected it would. The frame needed new timber, really.

The job done, Terry tugged out his penknife and made scratches on the window frame, such as boots might make; then he returned downstairs again to the manager's office. Propping up the torch and covering its glow with a sheet of pink blotting paper, he set to work on the oak door, deliberately chipping and scraping at the woodwork round the area of the lock. With his pocket screwdriver he loosened the screws on the lock clamp, closed the door, then hurled himself at it from the outside. The door smashed open, tearing the clamp half off in the process.

'So far, so good,' Terry murmured, glancing at his watch.

It was 11-15. He had to finish off as quickly as possible. Around midnight the transport men would arrive to take away the used films and deliver a new programme. As a rule they never went much beyond the front doors — they had a key to the building and were entirely trustworthy — but Terry did not intend to be anywhere in the building when they came, if he could help it.

He almost closed the door and went over to the safe, pulling out the note he had made of the combination. His rubber-gloved fingers caressed the knob gently. 5-R, 6-L, 2-R, 7-L. And at last a click. He pulled the heavy door open and smiled at the cash box perched on the top shelf where Madge Tansley had placed it. It was locked, of course, but it would not be so for long once Terry got it to his rooms —

A sound!

Terry jerked up his head, his pulses racing. It was a key in the front door lock! The transport men must have come long before time. Well, nothing to worry about. They would never come this far into the building: they had no need to.

Terry snapped out the torch and pushed the cash box into his jacket as best he could, working the lowest button into its hole. He got up, glided to the slightly open door, and listened . . . Queer. No sound of transit cases being dumped on the floor. No sounds at all, in fact.

Then he heard footsteps, so faint they were hardly audible on the strip of pile carpet, which ran down the centre of the foyer. A ghostly figure passed the dim crack of the door and went towards the staircase. Terry opened the door further and, in his endeavours to lean out, he forgot the cash box under his jacket. Its weight made it slide down. He made a frantic grab at it in the dark, missed, and it thudded to the rubberoid at his feet.

The footsteps on the stairs stopped. After a pause they resumed again, becoming louder as the intruder returned slowly to the foyer. Terry gave a wild glance about him. He saw a dim figure. He did not wait to ask questions but lunged out with the extinguished torch he was gripping. Just in time the figure jerked back and he missed. He tripped over the fallen cash box and fell sprawling. The impact as he hit the floor snapped the torch into brilliance.

Cursing to himself he swung the beam

round and it glared on to Vera Holdsworth, narrowing her eyes in the radiance. She was dressed just as she had been on leaving the cinema with Sid, in her light topcoat and silk scarf, her fluffy blonde hair uncovered.

'Well, if it isn't Terry!' she commented cynically, as at length she was able to distinguish him.

He got to his feet and the girl glanced down as her foot caught against the cash box on the rubberoid. She stooped to pick the box up but Terry snatched it first.

'Get in that office!' he breathed. 'Go on, damn you — get *in*!'

Vera hesitated, but a savage thrust of Terry's hand sent her stumbling backwards through the doorway. She brought up sharp, gasping, as she struck the roll top desk. There was fear on her face now, and Terry thrilled to it. He hated this girl, hated her more than anybody on earth. He was convinced that she was somehow responsible for all the troubles that seemed to be besetting him.

'What the hell are you doing here?' Terry demanded.

'That cuts both ways, doesn't it?' Vera snapped back at him. 'What's going on in here? You're — You're a thief!' she cried. 'You've stolen the cash box out of the safe!'

'I said: why are you *here*?'

'I came for my cigarette case.'

'You what?'

'Cigarette case! You deaf? I forgot it — left it in my uniform.'

Terry reflected over something; thcn he went to the safe door and closed it, spun the combination knob rapidly.

'You're stealing money, aren't you?' Vera asked, in vicious satisfaction. 'Kind of thing you would do! You've even got rubber gloves on to prevent fingerprints!'

Terry picked up the cash box and jammed it inside his jacket once more. Then he went close to the girl.

'Listen to me, Vera . . . ' His voice was quiet, deadly. 'You've caught me red-handed, and I'm not mug enough to deny it — but if you know what's good for you, you'll never say a word.'

'Likely, isn't it? Why, this is just the sort of chance I've been waiting for! To pay you for the way you hit me! I'll tell the boss when he gets back tomorrow — '

'Oh, no you won't! You see, nobody except you knows that I've come back here tonight. There's not a single clue to prove that I've had anything to do with this burglary. You have a passkey to the building; you're the head usherette with every opportunity to know the takings at the box office — and, if it comes to that, the combination of the safe. In a word, only one person is known to have come back here . . . *you!*'

Vera was silent, wrestling with the obvious truth.

'If you spill the beans and say you saw me, I'll deny it,' Terry went on. 'And you've no witnesses to prove what you say!'

'What you mean is, you're going to let me take the blame for this in any case?' Vera demanded.

'No. If you keep your mouth shut you've nothing to be afraid of. I've fixed everything so it looks like an outside job.'

Vera bit her lip. Then, 'what on earth did you want to steal the money for, anyway?'

'I'm not answerable to you for — '

Terry held up his hand sharply at a sudden commotion at the front doors. There was the sound of heavy feet, the crash of transport cases, and the unmusical strains of the latest rock 'n roll.

'Transport men,' Terry whispered, leaving a slight crack down the office door as he listened. 'Not a word! You're in this as much as I am — '

'But you've got the cash box. It's my one chance to — '

Terry jumped, smothering the girl's efforts to cry out. He clamped his hand with savage force over her mouth. He held on to her with savage tenacity as she fought and struggled. He only released her when the front doors had slammed and the men had gone. A moment or two afterwards there was the sound of their lorry grinding away up the street in first gear.

'Don't try and get smart!' Terry snapped. 'It won't do you any good . . . Now we're going upstairs and get that cigarette case of yours.'

Using his torch, they went up the

staircase together. He cast a light for her as she went into the staff room and across to the uniform she wore when on duty. In another moment she had brought the cigarette case into view. A powder compact, keys, and a wallet fell out onto the floor, mainly because Vera, flustered, whipped the uniform wrong way up in grabbing at it. Immediately she dived for the fallen articles, but Terry pushed her away.

'Just a minute!' he said slowly, turning the torch beam on the assortment. He stooped and picked up the wallet, looked inside it, and ran his thumb down a wad of notes. His eyes moved slowly to where Vera was standing, breathing hard.

'All right, it's *your* wallet!' she snapped, tossing her head.

'Yes, *my* wallet. And about fifty pounds here! And you had the blasted nerve to call *me* a thief!' Terry's voice mounted into fury. 'Why, you cheap little liar, this money is mine, and the wallet! I thought some wide boy had done the stealing, although I couldn't fathom how anybody else but you could have known how much money I'd got. You were the only one who did know: I took good care of that. I once thought it was you and then I decided you couldn't be that rotten — I was wrong! Five of these notes have got pencilled initials in one corner; I marked them myself to know how much money I'd got.'

Vera said nothing, but she was breathing hard.

'Where's the rest of it?' Terry blazed. Then as she did not answer he seized her arm and shook her violently. 'Where's the *rest* of it?'

'I . . . spent it.' Her reply was sullen, after a long interval. 'All right, I admit I took it, after the horse had lost. It was when you were lying on the grass with your back to me. The wallet was sticking out of your hip pocket. I knew the money would only go to the bookie, and I could think of lots of better uses for it. I put the money down for a fur coat . . . And what do you suppose you're going to do about it?'

'Nothing,' Terry answered slowly. 'Just nothing. In fact the position's perfect. If anything makes certain you'll keep your mouth shut, this does. In this cash box I've stolen there are about two hundred pounds — to make up for the two hundred you stole. I've got to pay that bookie, or take a beating, which I don't intend to do. I can't get back the money you've used, or prove anything. *But*, if the police find you've spent about one hundred and fifty quid on a fur coat and still have this fifty left they'll ask a few questions, won't they?'

Vera was silent. Terry hurled the wad of notes at her and they spewed in a shower at her feet.

'Take them, my bright one,' he sneered. 'One lot of two hundred pounds is the same as another, far as I'm concerned. I've got all I want and a guarantee of your silence . . . Incidentally, how do you intend to explain your fur coat to your mother and father?'

'I shan't until the winter. Its actual price is about three hundred pounds. All I've done is put a down payment . . . I'll have thought of an excuse when the dark weather gets here. I'll tell them I won a bet. They won't be too fussy.'

Terry was thoughtful for a moment or two, then he squatted down and scooped the money and odds and ends together.

'Time we got out of here,' he said curtly.

Vera collected her belongings and went in front of him down the staircase. In the manager's office he rid himself of the torch and left the damaged door swinging. In darkness he and Vera crossed the foyer and passed out by the front doors. Terry took off his rubber gloves as they came to the street.

'Better watch your step,' he warned, then without another word he went on his way.

3

Police investigation

As Terry had expected, Mrs. Gordon, his landlady, when he met her and her husband at breakfast the following morning, fully believed him when he said he had come in about half past ten the previous night after seeing Helen Prescott home.

No reason why they should not believe him. Though it was not a cast-iron alibi he considered it was perhaps good enough, if one should be needed. He did not even anticipate such an eventuality.

When he had had breakfast he went upstairs for the cash box he had smashed open and, whilst he knew Mr. and Mrs. Gordon were still at breakfast, he lowered the box by a piece of string into the back yard. This done, he left the house in the usual way, looking in on the old couple before he left — if only to reveal that he was not padded out by a large, concealed object.

Satisfied that the morning newspaper and the marmalade would keep the couple absorbed for at least another ten minutes, Terry dodged round to the back of the house, collected the cash box, and with it under his raincoat — which he carried on his arm — he made his way swiftly down the back entry which led to an old building site. Here he polished all fingerprints from the box and then buried it under a pile of brick ends and rubbish. Smiling to himself he continued on his way, arriving at the Cosy Cinema about nine o'clock.

That which he had anticipated had happened. He was met in the foyer by an excited doorman, and the staff of girls and cleaners was drifting up and down, talking or crowding about the smashed door of the manager's office.

'What goes on?' Terry asked in surprise, flattening down his unruly black hair.

'Burglary, that's what,' the doorman answered, his wind-inflamed eyes unusually bright. 'I found it first thing this morning when I got 'ere to open the place up. Lav'try window's bust in upstairs and the gaffer's door has bin broken down.'

'Oh?'

Terry allowed urgency into his movements. He hurried over to where the staff was crowding round the smashed door of the office.

'All right, all right, so there's been a burglary,' he said. 'Nothing we can do about it except call the police. Have you done that, Harry?'

The doorman shook his head. 'No. I waited to see what you said. Else the gaffer 'e'll be back this morning, won't he?'

'Should be, but we'd better advise the police just the same. They can start looking round — Oh, wait a minute! We'd better be sure first if anything's been stolen. The safe doesn't look any different and nothing else seems to have been taken. We'd better wait until Madge Tansley gets here. She's got the safe combination.'

An air of indecision settled on the group. Terry looked about him.

'We'll act fast enough when Madge comes,' he said. 'In the meantime don't forget you've got work to do — The cleaning goes on even if the place *has* been rifled.'

Terry caught a look from Vera Holdsworth . . . It was cold and cynical. She lighted a cigarette and turned away, duster in hand. Helen Prescott lingered behind for a moment, tightening the scarf about her black hair — then she went on her way.

Terry glanced down the foyer as Sid Eldridge and Billy arrived together. They paused by the doorway, heaved the waiting transit cases on their shoulders, and then continued the journey inwards.

'Rehearsal as usual, Terry?' Sid asked.

'You'd better run it yourselves,' Terry instructed. 'Keep a check on it and note the cues, changeovers, and any bad recording. I'm likely to be kept down here. I have to see the boss about a burglary.'

'Burglary!' Billy exclaimed.

'Boss's office, during the night. Somebody got in through the lavatory window.'

Sid and Billy exchanged wondering looks, then they went on up the staircase. The doorman came back across the foyer, trailing the vacuum suction pipe.

'Not much of a greeting for the gaffer, eh?' he reflected, scratching his chin. Grumbling to himself he went on his way; then Terry turned to Madge Tansley as she came in at the front door.

'Just a minute, Madge . . . ' Terry motioned her. 'There's been some trouble during the night. You'd better open the safe.'

'Trouble? Safe?' Just for the moment Madge Tansley looked anything but efficient. She seemed positively vacant.

Terry made the facts plain to her and it was sufficient to set her hurrying across the foyer into the manager's office. She opened the safe from the combination record in her notebook and then started back.

'Good heavens, the cash box has gone!'

'How much was there in it?' Terry demanded.

'About two hundred pounds — Here! Here's the return sheet.' Madge picked it up from the shelf below. 'Exactly two hundred and five pounds and ten shillings.'

'Mmm — that's bad.' Terry looked suitably troubled.

'But who on Earth could have done it?' the girl demanded. 'It's a combination safe and nobody knows the combination outside the boss and me.'

At her look of growing anxiety Terry patted her arm gently. 'Don't start getting steamed up, Madge! Take it easy.'

Terry stopped and turned as Mark Turner, the owner-manager, suddenly appeared from the foyer. He was a short, impeccably dressed man who gave the impression of being an expert with an electric razor.

'Hallo, Terry — morning, Miss Tansley.' He put his brief case on top of the roll top desk and drew off his wash-leather gloves. 'Is there — anything wrong?' he asked, in some curiosity.

'Yes, sir, I'm afraid there is.' With perfect calm Terry gave the facts. When he had all the details Turner frowned thoughtfully.

'That makes the fourth burglary we've had here,' he said, sighing. 'Apparently nothing is safe anymore. All right, I'll get the police. It's for them to deal with, not us . . . '

He picked up the telephone and Terry followed the cashier into the foyer. Thoughtfully, Terry went on his way up the staircase.

'Anything doing?' Helen Prescott asked him, as she dusted. 'I mean about the burglary.'

'Police are coming,' Terry answered her. 'And the boss is back to look after things.'

Terry went on his way to the winding room, content again in his own mind that his £205 was perfectly safe in his hip pocket. Just the same, when he had put his mackintosh on the peg he did not remove his jacket as he usually did. The tail of it covered his hip pocket, and the bulge therein.

'The thing now,' he murmured, 'is to show complete disinterest in the burglary. Never even mention it and pay complete attention to normal work. Right!'

He nodded to himself and went up the steps into the projection room. Sid was in the midst of rehearsal, running No. 2 machine and watching the screen in the cinema. He glanced round as Terry came in. Billy glanced up from lacing film into No. 1.

'Any news, Terry?' the youth asked eagerly. 'Have the flat-foots caught anybody yet?'

'They're not even here yet,' Terry answered. 'And anyway, we've more important things to do than bother about burglaries. How's it going, Sid?'

'Oh, not bad. Nice copy. Pretty long programme, though.'

Terry glanced about him. 'I'll go down in the Circle and see how it sounds. You know where I sit. If I'm wanted at all send Billy down.'

Terry departed. In a few moments he was on the front row of the Circle and appeared to be watching the screen and making the usual notes for the programme run. In truth, his thoughts were miles away, debating the £205 and the activities of the police, which would shortly commence . . . Before long his expectations were realized. The manager came up into the Circle, looking even shorter than usual beside the tall, powerfully-built Superintendent Standish of the local force, resplendent in his official uniform. Terry knew him well enough; He was hot stuff on fire regulations and had a gift for arriving at moments when films were in places where they shouldn't be.

'As you can see, Super,' Mark Turner said, 'there's no possible way in which a burglar could have got in up here. That lavatory window is the spot. No doubt of it.'

'Yes, so it seems,' the Superintendent agreed, looking around him. 'I just wondered, that's all. Sometimes an inside job can be faked to look like an outside one — Oh hello, chief! I didn't notice you sitting there.'

Terry glanced round and smiled. 'Good morning, Super. Just in the midst of a rehearsal.'

The manager glanced at the screen. 'Better let Sid do it, Terry,' he said. 'I want a word with you down in my office. The Superintendent would like to ask you a few questions.'

Terry felt his heart quicken, but he nodded calmly enough and got to his feet.

'Just as you wish, Mr. Turner.'

He followed the small and large figures down the wide staircase, passing Helen Prescott on the way. Though they exchanged glances, Terry hardly noticed her. He was wondering what on earth there could be to talk about. There was no clue he had left, nothing for the police to seize on to —

'Just a check up, chief,' the Super said, when they were in the office with the damaged door pushed to. 'I believe you've been in charge here during Mr. Turner's absence?'

'That's right,' Terry assented.

'And nobody else has ever been in this office without your being aware of it?'

'Why, no.' Terry's surprise was genuine. 'Usherettes have been in, of course, for torches and new batteries — but only when I've been here. And yesterday our head cashier came in to — '

73

'Yes, yes, to put money in the safe,' the Super interrupted. 'I've already taken a statement from Miss — er — '

'Tansley,' Turner said, leaning against the desk.

'Tansley. That's it. Anyway,' the Super went on, 'there's another point I want to take up. Namely — this.'

He picked up the ashtray from the small table beside the desk and held it forward. Terry looked at it fixedly . . . it was the stubbed three-quarter length of an oval Turkish cigarette. He had forgotten all about it until now. It was the one he had extinguished the morning before because he did not care for the exotic tobacco.

'I've told the Super there's only one person around here who smokes that kind of cigarette,' Turner remarked in his quiet voice, his eyes studying Terry's face. 'Sid Eldridge, of course. But the Super wants your verification.'

Terry found it hard to think straight. This unexpected spanner in the works had thrown things right out of gear.

'Well, chief?' Standish asked. 'Does the

second projectionist smoke this kind of cigarette, or not?'

'Yes, he does.' Terry gave a reluctant nod. 'But surely you are not thinking that he committed this burglary?'

'I'm not thinking anything. I'm just making routine enquiries, that's all. You say that as far as you know nobody ever came into this office unless you were in it? And that includes Eldridge?'

'Certainly it does. In fact nobody *could* come in. Outside of Mr. Turner I was the only one with a key.'

'I see. Then you can't explain how this cigarette got here?'

'No . . . ' Terry was not quite sure, but he fancied he saw suspicion drifting away from him. The Super pondered for a moment or two and then he nodded.

'Very well, chief, that's all. You might ask your second to come down and have a word with us, will you?'

'And if you don't mind, I'll have the office key back,' Turner said, holding out his hand.

Terry unhooked it from his ring and then left the office.

He still could not see how things were going to turn out. He did not in the least like the sudden twist in circumstances. When he got back to the projection room he gave the Superintendent's order and from Sid received a stare of amazement.

'What does he want *me* for?' Sid demanded, rubbing his mop of sandy hair.

'I've not the vaguest idea, but you'd better go and see. I'll take over the rehearsal.'

'I'll tell that uniformed old buzzard a thing or two,' Sid grumbled. 'Calling me off like this just when the show's getting to the interesting part.'

He lumbered out of the projection room and the spring door slammed shut behind him. Terry finished the rehearsal show, with Billy's assistance, but he had little idea after so many interruptions what it was all about.

He lounged across the box, hands in pockets, and went out on to the fire escape. The sun was bright and warm. Dim, startling thoughts were at the back of his mind. Vera Holdsworth, he felt sure, really *did* care for Sid. In fact she had admitted it at the racecourse. For another thing, Sid himself had said it was serious enough for him to think about getting an engagement ring. And if Sid ran foul of the police for the burglary, what then?

Would Vera stand by and let him be suspected — even jailed if circumstantial evidence added up to anything — or would she tell what she knew and risk the fact that Terry could not prove she had stolen his £200?

'Blast that Turkish cigarette!' Terry breathed, gripping the iron rail and staring over the agglomeration of back yards.

He turned with a sudden start at the slam of the projection room's spring door. Sid's ungainly figure came into view.

'Well?' Terry asked quietly, as Sid came out to him.

'It beats me!' Sid declared, frowning. 'I do believe that dimwit of a Super thinks *I* did it!'

Terry laughed derisively, even though

his nerves were taut.

'That's what I think,' Sid continued. 'But — Gosh, but he hasn't half got it in for me! Seems he's questioned most of the usherettes and all of them have brought up that business of yesterday morning when we had that row over Vera.'

Terry stared. 'But what the devil's that got to do with it?'

'Plenty! Remember me saying that you'd no right to toss around two hundred quid whilst I am pinching and scraping to get a house together for Vera and me?'

'Yes, I remember.'

'Well, the Super seems to think — though he didn't say so openly — that that might be a good reason for me wanting to pinch some cash!'

'Ridiculous!' Terry exclaimed, though his mouth was dry. There seemed to be a whole flock of things he had overlooked which were now popping up and confronting him menacingly.

'Mostly, it's that cigarette that makes things bad for me,' Sid went on deliberately. 'One of my Turkish ones. *I* didn't put it there, but the Super says I must have done. He also says I'm tough enough physically to have smashed in the office door. On top of that he says it wouldn't have been hard for me to get the safe combination from Madge Tansley.'

'But surely you've got an alibi for last night?' Terry demanded.

'No, I haven't.' Sid shook his untidy head worriedly. 'That's the rotten part of it. Before going home last night I went for a walk round to get some of the copper fumes out of my lungs. There is an hour I can't account for after leaving here. I saw Vera as far as her home and then strolled back to my own place by the longest way round.'

Terry surveyed the wilderness of back yards and the bricks and stones, which he had come to know with intimate detail.

'It's all circumstantial, Sid,' he said.

'I don't feel like trusting to that when there's one person who can clear me. I mean you!' Sid was silent for a moment. 'That Turkish fag must be the one I gave you some time ago. What I don't understand is why you didn't say so to the Super.'

'Matter of fact, I couldn't think straight for the moment.'

'Then it's about time you started remembering, isn't it?' There was a grimness in Sid's voice now and a hard glitter in his blue eyes. Terry hesitated for a moment, and then smiled. All of a sudden he wondered why he had been such an idiot. Of course!

If he proved the cigarette was one he had smoked that would lift all suspicion from Sid. Vera would thereby be silenced again because with Sid out of danger she would have no cause to speak.

'I'll clear it up right away,' Terry said, straightening himself. 'Believe me, Sid, I'd have explained sooner only I just didn't — '

'I know — you didn't think about it. All right. But for Pete's sake make them turn the heat off me!'

Terry gave a reassuring smile as he turned to go. 'Leave it to me!'

His smile faded, however, as he descended the stairs towards the foyer. He was going to clear Sid because he *had* to in order to make himself safe. But a larger and more complicated problem loomed: the very one he had hoped to keep hidden — the £200 he had lost on a race bet. He could not think how he had come to overlook the fact that the usherettes would be bound to testify as to the amount involved.

'You didn't overlook it,' he told himself. 'It would never have come up at all but for that Turkish cigarette. That involved Sid. The Super had got to find out if Sid had grounds for *wanting* to steal two hundred pounds. And now everything's falling to bits.'

Terry did his best to eradicate the lines of worry from his face as he knocked on the manager's office door. On being told to come in he found the manager and Superintendent seated in discussion.

'Yes, Terry?' Turner glanced up, his face serious and unsmiling.

'I've been thinking,' Terry said, pushing the door to. 'I just remembered something about that Turkish cigarette. It was one I smoked myself, then I stubbed it out because I didn't like it.'

'Oh?' Turner exchanged a glance with

the Super. 'And when was this, Terry?'

'Yesterday morning, when I was in here. Madge — Miss Tansley — came to put the money in the safe.'

'She doesn't remember the aroma of a Turkish cigarette,' the Superintendent commented. 'I've already made sure of that on the chance that it might have belonged to you.'

'She hardly could: I smoked it after she had gone. Sid gave me the cigarette, and as I say I stubbed it out because I didn't care for the flavour.'

Not a muscle moved on the Super's big, square-jawed face. His next comment was brief and to the point.

'Been a long time remembering it, haven't you?'

'Yes, I'm afraid I have,' Terry admitted. 'Just got crowded out of my mind with one thing and another.'

The Super reflected, and in spite of himself Terry flinched under the cold, probing eyes.

'Whilst you are here, chief, there's another matter I'd like to take up with you,' the Super resumed. 'From all accounts you did a spot of gambling at the races on Tuesday — to the tune of some two hundred pounds loss. Right?'

Terry felt the screw tightening.

'It's a mug's game,' the Super added surprisingly. 'And you're fortunate in that you have so much money to throw about. Who's your bookie?'

'George Naylor.'

'Naylor, eh? Mmm, I know that gent.'

'I don't see,' Terry said, making a tremendous effort, 'how you can attach the coincidence of my losing two hundred pounds to the money that has been stolen. I know it was thc same amount — in fact two hundred and five pounds — because Madge Tansley told me as much. But you don't think I robbed the safe, surely? I was at home when the burglary must have occurred.'

'Tell me something,' the Super said. 'Why are you trying to cover up for Sid Elbridge?'

'But I'm not — If you mean about that cigarette — '

'I do — and though I'm all for loyalty in its proper place, it's plain crazy when it obstructs the law.'

'Look,' Terry persisted, 'you can't mean that you don't believe me when I say I smoked that cigarette?'

'I think,' Turner put in quietly, 'that you'd better get back upstairs, Terry. Thanks for all you've told us.'

Terry went, more bewildered than he had been upon arrival.

He just did not know where he stood. Apparently the police believed that Sid was the culprit — and yet the thing Terry had expected, a direct question as to how he had had £200 with which to bet, had never been asked! Turner alone knew why. He was wary. Long experience as an employer had taught him just how much he could ask and do.

He had no authority for enquiring why an employee had two hundred pounds, even though he could wonder privately about it. It was the Superintendent's job to tackle a thing like that — but even he was holding off until he had a definite angle to follow up.

When he got back to the projection room Terry found Sid looking at him eagerly.

'Well, what happened? Did you clear me?'

'No. The Super wouldn't believe me.'

Sid's impulsive anger gushed to the surface. 'I've damned well had enough of this! I'm going to — '

'Just a minute!' Terry caught Sid's powerful arm and made him pause. 'It won't do you any good, Sid. Don't go off half cocked.'

With an effort Sid calmed down. 'Then who do you think did it?' he demanded. 'It could only have been somebody with a knowledge of the safe combination, and what outside person could possibly know that?'

'An expert burglar wouldn't need the combination for an ancient safe like that.' Terry answered. 'He could do it by touch. Frankly, I think we're both in something of a spot. We'd better keep quiet until we see what happens.'

4

Plan for murder

Immediately upon leaving the cinema at noon Terry hurried to George Naylor's, paid his £200 to that obese gentleman's grim satisfaction — and then went on to his rooms for lunch. He ate very little and had a hard struggle to keep his inner worries under control.

'Anything the matter, Terry?' Mrs. Gordon asked in concern, as he sat staring at his dinner.

He gave a start. 'Oh — er — ' He forced a smile. 'Trouble at the cinema, I'm afraid.'

'Oh . . . You mean the show didn't turn up on time?'

'Not that: the show's all right. There's been a burglary and since all of us are under suspicion it gets a bit disturbing.'

A sudden thought struck Terry. 'If the police should call here, Mrs. Gordon

— and they might — you won't forget to tell them that I got home at the usual time last night, will you?'

'Of course I'll tell them,' Mrs. Gordon promised, smiling. 'Now do get on with your lunch, Terry.'

Terry started on his meal, even though he had to force himself — then he set off for the cinema again, mentally holding his breath, for fear of what might assail him when he got there. Nothing did. Before he could ascend the staircase to the upper regions, however, he saw Vera Holdsworth bob into view from behind the glass doors leading to the stalls.

'Just a minute, Terry . . .'

'What do you want?' Terry stopped on the bottom stair.

She came closer to him and kept her voice low. 'I went home with Sid at lunch time. He told me what's been happening. The police think *he* committed that burglary.'

'I know. They can't prove it, though.'

'You bet they can't!' Vera's blue eyes were venomous. 'Sid's about the only person I've ever cared two hoots about, and if you think he's going to get nailed for something *you* did you can think again.'

'Getting a bit ahead of yourself, aren't you?' Terry asked. 'Nobody's accused him of anything yet.'

'If they do, I'll clear him!'

'And lay yourself open to a packet of trouble?'

Vera smiled unpleasantly. 'I've had time to think over what you said to me last night. Situation's altered a lot since then. The police know now that you lost two hundred pounds on the races. I got all the girls to lay that information on pretty thick, 'cept Helen Prescott. But then, she always is too good to live.'

'Go on,' Terry said ominously.

'I look at it this way,' Vera went on. 'If it comes to it, I'll tell the police that I found you stealing the cash box. I will also tell them that you had your own money pinched at the races — which they don't know about so far — and that will give them good reason for thinking that you'd need two hundred in a hurry by any possible means. You can't prove that *I* took your two hundred, and from the way I'll talk they won't suspect that I ever could — anymore than you did.'

'And if I tell them that you planted one hundred and fifty for a fur coat out of the two hundred you stole from me, what do you think would happen?' Terry demanded. 'They'll ask you if it is so, and the name of the firm to whom you gave the order for the fur coat. Your goose will be cooked to a turn.'

'Perhaps.' Vera leaned against the post at the base of the handrail. '*Perhaps*! I've thought that one out, you know. On the one hand I could refuse to answer the question, and they couldn't force me to answer it. On the other hand I could say that I'd taken the money from home.'

'You could — what?' Terry found it impossible to fathom the depths of the girl's scheming mind. 'Where would you get one hundred and fifty from, at home? Your folks aren't that rich, are they?'

'No they're not — worse luck, but dad *is* the secretary and treasurer of the bowling club. I know he has quite two hundred pounds in the house at this very moment. The new subscriptions are just in, and he won't be handing them over for another fortnight — or even looking at them. I'm simply saying that if it became necessary — but not otherwise — I'd take the hundred and fifty of that money as easy as that, and say I spent it on a fur coat. That would cut the ground from under your feet, wouldn't it?'

'Perhaps. Wouldn't do you any good, though. Your dad would certainly give you in charge.'

'You don't know my dad,' Vera murmured. 'All he'd do would be to find the necessary money somewhere else, give me a talking to, and let it go at that. He wouldn't dare say too much. You see, I know something about dad, and he wouldn't like me to talk it out loud.'

'So that's where your vile streak comes from?' Terry blazed, and Vera's expression changed.

'You shut up, Terry!'

Terry gave a contemptuous smile. 'With such a marvellous plan worked out, why don't you adopt it?'

'Because I'm not such a fool as to put

myself in a spot if I can avoid it. I'll only do it if the police pick on Sid.'

Terry set his mouth and went on up the stairway. The girl called something uncomplimentary after him, but he did not hear the words . . . He found that Sid and Billy had already arrived by the fire escape route and were in the projection room lacing up the machines with film for the afternoon matinee. He could hear them exchanging argument as he took off his jacket. Finally he went up to the projection room to join them.

Sid waited until Billy had departed to his usual haunt in the winding room below — then he walked out onto the fire escape where Terry was standing gazing into the hot afternoon sunlight.

'Terry,' he said moodily, 'I've got butterflies in the stomach after that confounded burglary. If only something would happen! I'll lay evens the police think I did it. Why don't they do something?'

Terry was silent for a moment, then: 'I met Vera as I came in. She was telling me that you'd told her all about it — that the police suspect you.'

'Sure I told her. No reason why I shouldn't, is there?'

'I suppose not. But do you think she'll keep it to herself? Frankly, I don't. Or perhaps you like the idea of scandal and gossip being spread through the staff?'

Sid shook his head. 'As usual, you've got Vera weighed up all wrong. She won't say anything about me. We're too fond of each other for that.'

Terry raised one shoulder and then lowered it. There was a negative expression on his handsome face.

'Look, Terry, you won't like this,' Sid exclaimed suddenly, 'and it's no kind of talk to hand out to a workmate, but — Well, at lunch time I got to thinking. *You* didn't do it, did you? To recover the two hundred quid you lost on that horse?'

Terry's impulse was to swing round in outraged fury. Then he checked himself and said quietly, 'Don't get such damned silly ideas, man!'

'Sorry.' Sid rubbed the back of his thick neck. 'Just occurred to me that you had motive and opportunity. I wouldn't blame you if you did. Being in a spot goads one to queer antics sometimes.'

Terry turned, facing Sid squarely. 'You sound as though you think I *did* do it!'

'Not now.' Sid gave an awkward grin. 'Thanks for taking it the right way. That's the worst of me — I speak on impulse.'

'You like Vera quite a lot, don't you?' Terry asked.

'You bet I do! She's got everything I look for in a girl. Looks, spirit, and she's as straight and outspoken as the day.'

Terry spat casually over the iron rail to the concrete path far below.

* * *

The matinee was half over when Superintendent Standish came back to the cinema, to become immediately closeted with Turner.

'Well?' Turner asked, when cigarettes had been lighted.

'Obviously the theft was an inside job. That broken window is just so much eyewash. Further, no thief in his right senses — and having the delicacy of touch to open this safe — would ignore the booking office in which, as we know, there was about eighty pounds. That money was only in a flimsy drawer and the door of the booking office wouldn't worry a thief after this office door. Further, if we assume for one moment that Elbridge was the inside worker, we can be certain that he wouldn't be such an idiot as to smoke a Turkish cigarette and leave it in the ashtray. I know criminals make mistakes, but not such blatant ones as that.'

'Sid Elbridge is a quiet, steady worker,' Turner said. 'A bit blundering in some things, perhaps, and quick tempered — but I'd trust him with thousands if I had to. He didn't do this job, Super.'

'You merely anticipate me,' the Super smiled. 'I'm quite sure he didn't, having weighed him up. To my mind, there isn't the slightest doubt that the thief is Terry Lomond.'

Turner knocked the ash of his cigarette gently into the brass tray. He looked up to meet Standish's grim eyes.

'You think so, eh? I'm not saying that

I'm surprised. Not because I think that Terry has criminal tendencies — but he is rather a queer chap to assess, you know. He seems very quiet, and I imagine he thinks I'm completely fooled by it. But I'm not.'

Standish nodded slowly. 'For the moment, Mr. Turner, it looks as though he has committed the perfect crime, in that so far there isn't any real evidence against him. As you know, there isn't a clue in this office to show he's the culprit. The fingerprint men were here in the lunch hour, but their findings simply gave us a blur of prints of all shapes and sizes. Technically, no use at all. Whether Lomond used gloves or not we don't know, but we *do* know that his finger-prints are no more in evidence than anybody else's.'

'Knowing Terry, I think he would wear gloves,' Turner said.

'Further,' the Super continued, 'from Miss Tansley's statement I consider it quite possible that the thief could have watched her open the safe, and made a note of the combination whilst she did so.

She told him how much money there was before putting it in the safe. By that time he could have realized it might be worth his while to steal the cash. Miss Tansley was not accustomed to the combination: for that reason she would operate slowly, which suited Lomond perfectly. And lastly, there is the exceedingly damning point that at the races on Tuesday, as we know, Lomond lost two hundred pounds, about the same amount as that which was stolen.'

'True enough,' Turner agreed, pondering.

'You will recall that I asked him the name of his bookie. I went to see George Naylor this afternoon. At noon today Lomond paid him two hundred pounds and — note this! — Lomond could not pay up on the day of the race because he had had his wallet stolen. There we have our motive! Two hundred pounds lost, so he stole two hundred to make up the loss rather than have the bookie start hounding him. Unfortunately, the notes were not specially marked, so whether or not they came from here we'll never know. I went to the chief's lodgings, which address you gave me, and his landlady insisted at first that he came in at his usual time last night. When I pressed her, however, it seems she merely *assumed* that he did. She did not actually see him come in since she and her husband had retired.'

The Superintendent sat back in his chair. He considered for a moment.

'I had no warrant to search his bedroom, but I asked the good lady if I might look round. She was quite willing and told me that the chief had said we might call. I looked, but there was no sign of the cash-box. It may turn up somewhere: I've got men looking — but even if it does I doubt if it will do us any good.'

'And that's the whole story?' Turner asked.

'As near as I can piece it together, yes. Motive, opportunity, and the brains to carry the thing through.'

'About that Turkish stub — Do you suppose Terry planted it there to involve the second?'

'Do you?' the Superintendent asked deliberately.

'No, I don't. I don't think Terry would do a thing like that. He may be erratic — and in this case even criminal — but he is not a sneak. I think that is why he came down and said the cigarette is his responsibility. Either that, or else Sid made him come down and admit it.'

'Well, there it is,' Standish said, sighing. 'You can't very well prefer charges because there's no evidence — but that doesn't mean that there won't be. We'll watch him constantly.'

Turner sat musing for a few moments. 'I wonder,' he said finally, 'why Terry resorted to theft? I can only assume it was because gambling was involved, and he knows how I feel about that sort of thing . . .'

He came to a decision. 'I shan't fire him, Super. I shan't say anything at all. There are other considerations to this business. If he left me I'd be in quite a mess. He knows every trick and twist on the technical side — far more than Sid. If I lost him I'd lose far more than two hundred pounds in bookings from dissatisfied patrons. You see my point?'

'Up to you,' Standish said, picking up his uniform cap. 'The moment I alight on anything satisfactory I'll get in touch with you!'

* * *

If the genial, easy-going Mark Turner had wanted to devise the finest form of needle-pointed torture he could not have done better than choose the silence on which he had decided.

To Terry and Sid, both of them desperately anxious to know how events were working out during the hours they were chained to the running of the show, the lack of information was sheer anguish . . .

Terry did everything mechanically. In his mind's eye he pictured the manager's office. He saw the Superintendent and Turner talking together, no doubt discussing information gained.

'Reel five and six,' Sid announced, lacing up.

'Five and six, check,' Terry muttered.

Somewhere out there in the Circle, no doubt on that confounded tip-up seat with her back against the handrail, would be Vera. Terry peered through the porthole at an angle and could faintly see her in the red safety light. She was seated exactly as he had expected. The dirty little — !

His task done for the moment, Sid mooched out on to the fire escape, went down the four steps to the 'bridge,' and lighted a Turkish. After a while Billy sneaked out of the winding room emergency door and came to join him.

'Gimme a light,' he said, and pulled out a crumbly fag end which smelled of amyl-acetate.

Sid contemplated the youngster and smiled enviously to himself.

Billy was hot, cheerful, and filthy dirty. He always was when at work — but he had not a care in the world, except how large his tea would be. After a moment, Billy eased himself on to the top rail and locked his toes under the middle rail. He smoked contentedly, oblivious to his precarious position.

'You're a confounded little idiot,' Sid said critically, after a moment or two. 'If you got dizzy for a moment and your foot slipped you'd drop a hundred and fifty feet to that concrete down there. We'd need a shovel to scrape you up.'

'Wouldn't matter,' Billy shrugged. 'I wouldn't have to keep washing my neck if I broke it.'

'When did you start washing it?' Sid asked dryly.

They were both silent for a while. From inside the projection room the monitor speaker recording the sound chattered noisily.

'No, no, you mustn't do that! I won't let you.'

'Dearest, I must. Don't you realize that I've waited years for this moment? You and I are together — at last.'

'Aw, nuts,' Billy scowled, making a disrespectful noise. 'It stinks!' Then, caught by a sudden thought, he looked pensively at the cast iron grating which formed the floor of this turn in the fire escape — a turn better known as the 'bridge.' Through the latticed metalwork the entry far below was visible.

'Know something?' Billy asked.

'What?'

'The floor of this bridge is in two sections. Two squares of grating.'

Sid stared. 'So what? I've known that for years.'

'I was just thinking. Be a bit tough if somebody took 'em away one night and we came barging down in the dark to find there just wasn't any floor! Blimey! We'd look like fried eggs when we hit the concrete.'

'Hey, you out there!' yelled Terry's voice. 'Strike up!'

Sid dived up the steps to the projection room. He just caught the machine changeover in time, then he gave Terry a queer look.

'Didn't allow me much time, did you?'

'Sorry,' Terry apologized. 'I must have been day dreaming.'

Without doubt Vera would speak if things got tough for Sid. In that case, what was the way out? There was none except —

Terry started lacing film, into his machine.

'Reel seven and eight,' he called out mechanically.

'Seven and eight. Check.'

Even removing Vera before she had a *chance* to speak!

Terry paused in the act of threading film over the top sprocket. He was startled for a moment that such a thought had never occurred to him. One just couldn't remove a girl as casually as that . . . Terry stopped with the loop of film in his fingers . . . He racked the frame into position and snapped the gate shut.

Removal meant only one thing . . . Murder!

'You're going nuts,' he told himself, and whilst he recarboned the arc he thought further.

Murder and accidental death, are two different things. Naturally, he could not go out into the Circle with a knife and bury it in Vera's heart. That was only the first and rather ludicrous thought. A thing like killing isn't done straight off like that if you expect to get away with it. Planning — like the burglary. Great care! So nobody could ever tell . . .

Terry finished carboning and went out on to the fire escape, to think — hard. He was surprised to find that he was perspiring freely. Could only be the reaction from his thoughts. The box wasn't above seventy with its fan cooling.

Murder! Well, death, anyway. That didn't sound quite so bad. But was it worth the risk? He did not know even now what the police were going to do about the burglary. They *might* accuse Sid, in which case Vera would start talking. They might even accuse him — Terry — which would be just as bad. But how could they accuse him? He had not left behind a single clue.

Sid, on the other hand, had said he wanted money. He had no alibi. There was the Turkish cigarette —

'They must be getting the evidence ranged against him!' Terry beat his fist gently on the rail. 'That's what they're doing. That's why they're so quiet. Once they've got it they'll arrest him, and I'll be in a jam. But only if Vera speaks! She just hasn't *got* to speak. She's the only one who knows. With her out of the way there isn't a soul who can prove a thing . . . '

When the matinee was over Sid and Billy left for their tea by the fire escape route. It was quicker and saved them having to wait for the patrons to get clear before they could leave by the front entrance.

Terry, though, was in no hurry. For one thing he usually had tea at the café across the road, and for another before he dared to contemplate such a thing as murder — no, accidental death — he wanted to meditate and be sure if the act was justified. He must try and find out something, try and find how the police were faring — and now seemed to be as good a time as any.

He came down into the foyer by the main staircase from the Circle, moving with the scattering of patrons who had been at the matinee. As he had expected, Turner was in position at a corner of the foyer, immaculate in his lounge suit, beaming and bowing like a mechanical toy. Terry waited until the last patron had departed, then he went across to where

Turner was standing.

'Not a bad turn up for a hot day,' Turner commented, smiling, and if he read anything in Terry's taut, handsome face he gave no indication of it.

'No, sir, not at all bad,' Terry agreed. 'Something I wanted to ask you. About the burglary — '

'Yes?' Turner waited.

'Did the police get any further?'

'I had the Superintendent here this afternoon.'

'Oh . . . How far has he got?'

'I suppose,' Turner said, smiling, 'that you're uneasy because of the suspicion cast on the staff? I shouldn't worry, if I were you — Oh, Miss Gatty, I'll take the torches.'

Turner walked across to where Kathleen Gatty was standing with an armful of flashlamps. Terry looked after him hotly.

'I nearly mistook you for a cutout for next week's show!'

Terry gave a start. He had hardly noticed that Helen Prescott had come up behind him, changed from her cinema uniform into a summer frock.

106

'I'm having tea across the way today,' she said. 'Mother and dad are out, and sis is going out with the boy friend — so there's no point in my going home. You have tea across there, don't you?'

'Yes,' Terry assented absently.

Helen looked at him in surprise. 'What's the matter? Don't you *want* your tea? I know I do.'

'I — er — ' Terry forced himself to grin. 'I'm sorry, Helen. I wasn't with you, for the moment — But surely you don't want to have tea with me? I thought you'd sworn off me.'

'I never said we weren't still friendly, did I?'

Terry took her arm. 'Okay, what are we waiting for?'

They left the cinema together and crossed the road to the café — a small and by no means tidy place where the surroundings were drab, but the food was good and plentiful.

Helen insisted on talking, so Terry was compelled to answer.

'What's the matter with you today?' she asked at length, puzzled. 'What are you

107

looking solemn about? Here am I giving you the chance to get to know me better — and vice versa and you haven't answered above three of my questions!'

'I apologize. I've got things on my mind — chiefly the burglary.'

Terry glanced sharply towards the café window. There was a constable outside, looking in. Terry watched him intently. When at last the constable moved Terry felt a little trickle of perspiration starting from his forehead.

'Now what?' Helen demanded. 'Why on earth should that bobby looking in here give you goose-pimples?'

'Just nerves,' Terry said.

Throughout the remainder of the meal he took good care to be more attentive, and during the walk afterwards, before they returned to the cinema for the evening performance, he was in a good humour.

The mood faded somewhat when, upon entering the foyer with Helen, Terry saw Mark Turner standing there. He must have come back unusually early from tea. He motioned Helen towards him and good manners forbade Terry lingering. He went on his way, frowning.

'Does Terry mean anything to you, Helen?' Turner asked.

'Did you say — Helen?' She looked surprised for the moment.

'Forgive the liberty, but this is off-duty time. I came back early. Miss Gatty told me you were not going home to tea today when I asked which girl would be back first. I'd have liked to have taken you to the Silver Grill, but when I came out of the office after putting away the torches you'd gone.'

'You're — you're very kind.' Helen coloured slightly.

'Don't take it the wrong way,' Turner smiled. 'After all, we've been very good friends ever since you first came here.'

'I'm sure we have,' Helen responded, finding it rather difficult to know what to say.

'Spend much time with Terry?' Turner asked casually.

Helen shrugged. 'Very little. Today it just happened that both of us were going to the same café for tea.'

'I see.'

In the meantime, Terry had reached the winding room, and he was in a sullen mood. He tugged off his jacket impatiently and stood scowling thoughtfully at the rewinding bench.

'No doubt of it, I'd be a damned fool to try and blink the fact,' he muttered. 'Turner's crazy about Helen, just as I've always suspected. Vera turned out to be a two-timing thief, and Helen's stringing me along as well as the boss.'

He felt in a reckless, bitter mood. The remembrance of Vera returned to him. For the time being he had pushed into the back of his mind the realization that he was going to 'remove' her. Now he recalled it, and he bit his lip as he tried to think of a way.

'There isn't anything that's safe,' he told himself, still staring at the bench. 'And I certainly can't deal with her in the cinema. If I tried anything outside it would simply be common murder and the police would get me, sure as fate. But if she talks, which she *will* . . . '

Impatiently he broke off his speculations

110

as Sid and Billy returned from tea.

'Find out anything about the burglary?' Sid asked.

'Nothing that helps,' Terry answered.

He did not refer to the matter again, and because of his own sobering speculations Sid did not speak much either. For the next half hour both he and Terry attended to routine matters and, promptly at 7-30, the show began.

Terry opened with the news and watched it moodily. He merely had the interest of a technician in his performance. In the reflection from the projector beam stabbing across the darkened cinema he could see Vera sitting on the tip-up seat, her back wedged against the handrail, her face turned towards the screen.

Terry tightened his lips. There *must* be a way — !

The news finished. The comedy came and went —

Then an idea struck Terry. It smote him with cold, deadly certainty as he turned to the dimmer-wheel, which brought the six massive houselights into being. Vera was just stirring from her tip-up seat, preparatory to serving ices. At this moment Terry noticed something he had never observed before. Directly over the tip-up seat — or so it seemed from the angle of the projection room — was one of the houselights!

A slow smile came over Terry's face. He began to realize at last how Vera Holdsworth was going to die.

* * *

Beyond commenting on routine matters, Terry hardly spoke at all during the run of the feature picture. In the eighteen-minute periods when he was not running his machine, he wandered on to the fire escape and stood musing. A lot of factors had now to be taken into account. It looked — only *looked* — as though the rearmost houselight hung *directly over* the tip-up seat. Being fitted to the staircase panelling, the seat was separated from the nearest row of the audience by a distance of about nine feet to one side — the side opposite the tip-up seat — and about six feet on the other side, on which side the tip-up was fixed.

That meant that if a houselight globe came down — *the* houselight globe — it would not hit any member of the audience, but it *would* hit Vera, dead on! It would kill her — if not immediately, then very quickly.

Terry pressed finger and thumb to his eyes. His pulses were racing and his mouth felt dry. He had seen psychopaths on the screen many a time: he had never realized, nor did he even now, that they might have something in common with himself. Was it worth risking murder? Would it not be better to risk imprisonment for theft rather than try and kill the girl? But who would ever be able to prove that he *had* killed her? Nobody! Not even Scotland Yard, provided he worked cleverly.

He had to have the cinema to himself. He had to explore and find out the facts of the situation. With this in mind he complained, when taking over the running of his machine again, that it had developed a fault.

'Fault?' Sid repeated, and looked

through his own porthole onto the screen. 'Don't see anything wrong with the picture.'

'You're not likely to. I think it's the take-up that's giving trouble,' and Terry kicked the bottom spool box significantly.

'Well, it's no surprise,' Sid said. 'I've asked you often enough for replacements on those machines and you always fob me off. About time something *did* go wrong. Maybe we'll get some action.'

'I can soon fix it,' Terry said. 'I'll stay after the show tonight and have a go at it.'

The show ended at 9-50 and Terry nodded a casual goodnight to Sid and Billy as they departed. He listened to their feet going down the stone steps — they did not use the fire escape after dark since it was too dangerous — heard the door slam at the bottom; then he went up into the projection room again and hung about for a while until he got the signal over the buzzer to kill the houselights. This he did, and knowing that by now Turner would be in his office Terry picked up the direct-extension 'phone and pressed the button.

'Yes?' came Mark Turner's voice.

'I'm staying behind tonight, sir,' Terry said. 'I've got trouble with one of the machines, and I must get it right for the matinee to tomorrow. There might not be time in the morning with Billy having his day off.'

'Up to you,' Turner responded, and rang off.

Terry waited until everybody had gone, then he descended into the foyer and bolted the doors. If anybody returned and complained of being unable to enter he could always say that, being far away in the projection room, he had thought it wisest to bolt the doors — considering the burglary there had been.

This done he went with a lighted torch down the smoky, hot abyss of stalls to the door at the right hand side of the stage. Beyond the doorway was a narrow, wood-walled passage. On one side of it was the one-time orchestra pit. He went past it to a cat ladder and climbed until he came to the huge false roof space between the cinema ceiling and the roof proper. The space here was twelve feet high and a switch brought a string of 60-watt lamps into brilliance, illuminating an area of beams, plaster, and lath.

On here were also the fan chambers, the water tanks, and the winches, which held the houselights. Terry walked along the thick plank, which led to the furthermost — backmost — lamp on the left.

Carefully he disconnected the plug that put the lamp in circuit with the mains; then he released the winch-ratchet and braced himself. As he slowly allowed the winch handle to turn, the nine-stranded steel hawser cable holding the heavy lamp fixture creaked and twanged as the entire lamp descended into the Circle below.

Practically from memory Terry knew that nine turns would bring the lamp to a halt. He was right. At the ninth turn the wire became slack as the lamp obviously rasped on something below. He fixed the ratchet, returned downstairs and sped into the Circle where he switched on the solitary cleaning light in the roof.

The entire massive fixture had come to rest lopsidedly on the floor below the tip-up seat. Had the seat been down, instead of pressed back flat against the panelling, the light fixture would have been resting on it. And if somebody — Vera for instance — had been on the seat . . .

Terry's gaze travelled the length of the steel wire to the wooden rose in the ceiling, through which the wire vanished to join the winch drum above. Thoughtfully, his gaze returned to the lamp and its heavy oxidized fixture.

Now what? He had established beyond doubt that if the lamp — or any part of it — came down it would crash on top of Vera as she sat on the tip-up. There was a further established fact that the lamp in every particular was far bigger than a human head, so the chance of a misfire was almost impossible. Yet again there was the fact that Vera, owing to the handrail wedging on her back, was always forced to sit about eight inches away from the panelling. In a word, a sitting target. Provided she was seated on that tip-up seat, nothing could save her.

Accident? Yes, accident!

In that case the *whole fixture* must not come down because that would never look like an accident. The law would never accept the theory that a nine-stranded steel cable in perfect condition — checked every two months by the police department — had given way. Filing or hacksawing it would not do, either. For one thing it would leave traces that the forensic laboratory would be quick to identify; and for another there would be no way of determining when such a 'doctored' wire would snap. It *must* be at a time when Vera was on the seat — during a show.

'The whole fixture's definitely too much of a good thing,' Terry told himself. 'What else have we?'

As he knew, the globe was in two sections, two big hemispheres of exceptionally heavy opal glass, the lower hemisphere being heavier than the upper. The upper hemisphere was a fixture, sealed in by curved bands of oxidized metal. The lower half was held with three large turnscrews, the tips of which fitted under the lipped edge of the hemisphere.

To remove the lower hemisphere the screws had only to be unthreaded and so lay bare the bulb and socket within.

Turnscrews . . . Terry went down on his knees and turned them gently. They were fairly easy to twist, as indeed they ought to be. They were not screwed too tightly for fear that the glass, when expanding from the bulb's heat, cracked from lack of room.

Turnscrews . . .

If something could turn the screws without anybody being near them! If something could *loosen* them! If only one of them moved too far back, the lower half of the globe would come down. All three in alignment was the only thing that kept the lower half of the globe in place. For years Terry had insisted that they were dangerous fixtures . . . That fact might be useful. If one did come down nobody could say he hadn't issued a warning often enough.

But how to make the screws turn . . . ?

5

Pattern for murder

Terry pulled down the tip-up seat, sat on it, and lit a cigarette. He gave himself up to hard thought. One thing would turn them, and that was vibration. Vibration! He recalled that, during the war years, when the cinema had been in danger from bombs, the authorities had ordered that the turnscrews be secured with sealing wax so that anti-aircraft fire or bombing would not affect the screws. There had been the added order of wire netting to be fastened under the globes and up to the fixture itself to catch any globe fragments if splintered. These precautions had gone at the war's end, but —

Vibration *would* turn them. And since they could not turn any nearer the glass they would turn the other way — unravel along the thread —

Vibration!

Terry sat a long time before the dawn of an idea struck him, and that idea was born of a scientific fact. Up here, in the Circle, in a direct line with the backwardly-tilted loudspeakers behind the screen, the vibration travelled in a straight line. Technically speaking, the sound vibration was at its highest peak at the back of the Circle. Here! This spot! And around the houselight, when it was in its normal position. And also around the twin houselight on the other side of the ceiling.

Bass notes!

Bass notes reverberated with such force on the glass of the projection room portholes that the glass itself rattled sometimes. There was certainly an impact from the disturbed airwaves. But these of themselves would never be sufficient to move screws. It demanded a really high-powered *sustained* vibration until the screws, agitated by it, moved back-wards along their threads because they could not press any farther forwards, until finally their grip on the globe lip slipped.

Then — !

Terry crushed out his cigarette and put the remaining half in his case. He trod the ash into the carpet. His misdirected, scientific mind was at grips with the problem now. This would be no blood-and-thunder crime but a skilful execution of scientific truth. A sustained vibration had to be produced and it had to come from the screen's loudspeakers. And it had only to affect one houselight globe. *This* one.

'As to that,' he mused, 'the other globes are all fairly tightly fastened, and the weight of the lower hemisphere holds the screws firm. I doubt if vibration would shift 'em. But if on this one I loosened the screws until only a hair's breadth separated them from the edge of the glass, I'd be all right. Since the vibrations must somehow be devised from the hall speakers, that means it can only operate when the cinema is dark and the houselights extinguished . . . '

He thought for a moment. 'In that case, I can loosen the screws to the very limit of safety. As the globe gets hot it will expand and the danger will be lessened.

As it cools it will shrink and then the danger will return. The limit of coolness, according to my reckoning, will be about twenty minutes after the lamp has been switched off. That means we shall have got to the Fitzpatrick Travelogue in the programme. Ten minutes news and ten minutes comedy. *Then*, if a vibration could somehow be brought to bear, the cooled metal would be in its most 'sympathetic' state. Vibration would jar the screws over the hairline and — down she'll come!'

Terry felt his heart thudding with the intensity of his thoughts. He knew two things. He had got to loosen the screws to danger point — he even thought of oil and then abandoned the idea since oil would leave filmy traces — and the vibration, whatever it was to be, must happen when the Travelogue film was running. But how could a vibration be produced?

For a long time he meditated, and arrived at no conclusion. At his rooms he had books on sound and supersonics, which embraced the entire field of

123

audible and inaudible sound. Perhaps there might be an answer there. This was a scientific problem, utterly apart from the normal run of crimes. Something that nobody could ever solve once the thing was accomplished. If only he could work out the scientific theory struggling in the back of his mind for recognition, he had the practical side in his grasp. And he must work fast, before Vera could say anything.

He left the Circle, returned to the false roof, and wound the houselight back into position. When he returned to the Circle to look at the globe there was no clue to show that it had been lowered, except for the fact that at the moment it was swinging like a pendulum. He waited until finally it became motionless, then he sat on the tip-up and stared directly above him. All he could see was the white circle of the lower hemisphere floating in the void like a pale moon, some fifteen feet above. Certainly it would not hit anybody in the audience when it came down.

Shutting all further thoughts from his mind for the moment, Terry confined his attention to switching off lights and making preparations for departure. Then he unbolted the front doors, locked them again on the outside, and left the cinema.

Mr. and Mrs. Gordon had gone to bed when he reached his rooms, but as usual a supper had been left for him and he prepared his own hot drink. As he ate and drank he studied the book he had brought from his collection upstairs. He read:

The human voicc varies between 60 and 1,300 vibrations a second, covering four and a half octaves . . .

'Technically,' Terry muttered, chewing steadily, 'the cinema sound varics between forty and fifty decibels. And that is the point. If I were to raise the sound for a moment it would only be a noise, *not* a vibration. Besides, it would be suspicious — suddenly making the sound higher for no apparent reason. That won't do . . . The thing is, the higher the pitch of the sound the greater the rate of vibration.'

The higher the pitch, the greater the vibration. Terry stopped chewing. 'Of course! And the highest range an average human ear can detect is 20,000 vibrations a second. Above that,' he mused, 'is the supersonic range. Inaudible sound, but there just the same. Detectable by instruments but not by the ear — and the higher up the scale it is the more vibratory power it has. Suppose we had sixty to eighty thousand vibrations a second. What would we get then . . . ?'

He knew perfectly well what he would get — an inaudible but powerful vibratory wave, which, striking the loosened screws of the houselight globe, would undoubtedly make them turn in their threads. He sat with his supper forgotten, debating the beauty of the idea. Nobody would hear the sound, and yet it would be devastatingly effective. Or would it be *too* effective and shatter the glass of the globe — or perhaps both globes in line with the screen? That would ruin the whole thing. He could only tell by experiment . . .

So the final and greatest problem of all: how to create a supersonic wave with the show running normally as well. Terry had gone to bed and been there for an hour, wakeful and brooding, before he began to grasp another technical fact culled from his long experience as a projectionist and sound engineer.

'Some films,' he told himself, 'produce a high-pitched sound, almost inaudible, in addition to the normally recorded track.'

He had come across such films in his experience, films which, by some accident in processing, or carelessness in running, had had their sound tracks punctured with spaced dots at regular intervals along the side of the track itself. These punctures, racing through the sound gate at the film speed of 90 feet a minute, had produced a continuous high-pitched whine in the speakers, caused by the persistence of sound from one puncture to another, much the same as a stick swept along iron railings produces one metallic sound, instead of individual notes as each iron railing is momentarily struck.

'Sprocket hum', the curse of many a projectionist, might for once be turned to advantage. In Terry's experience, the dots that had caused this intense high frequency note had been about an eighth of an inch apart. But suppose some were made much closer together on a reel of film? The nearer the punctures to each other the higher the pitch produced. It might be possible to get the dots so close to each other that the sound they made would soar into the supersonic range and become inaudible.

The idea fascinated Terry so much he wanted to try it out immediately, but he checked the impulse. If by any chance he were caught at the cinema in the early hours of the morning his devotion to duty might appear a little over-zealous to say the least of it. So he stayed where he was.

On the morrow the inquisitive Billy would be off for the day and Sid would be taking over the youth's work — cleaning the projection room and the machines. During that time Terry decided he could satisfy himself on certain points. There was, he remembered, a Christmas carol film from last year's festive season, which had 'sprocket hum', though not severe enough to interfere with the normal recording. He could measure the distance apart of the holes that caused the hum. If there was room, he could double or treble the number of punctures.

How?

Well, there were many small gear wheels in the junk pile in the winding room, some no bigger than a sixpence and perfectly cast with a multitude of fine, sharp teeth. All he had to do was fix a spindle through the wheel and secure it to a handle. Then he could run the wheel along the edge of the sound track, using strong pressure, as a cook might cut pastry with a wheeled pastry cutter. The teeth would leave perfect punctures at mathematically spaced intervals.

Terry fell into a doze, absorbed with the technical side of the problem. That it was aimed at the cold-blooded murder of an unsuspecting girl, however unpleasant she might be, was furthest from his considerations . . .

When he arrived at the cinema the following morning he found Sid in the winding room, mixing film cement. There was an over-powering odour of pear drops in the air.

'I've a mind to go down and ask the

boss how I stand,' Sid said, taking the subject of the burglary so much for granted he did not even bother to lead up to it.

'Up to you,' Terry shrugged. 'How much do you think you'll get out of it, though? He won't say anything unless he has proof. All he'll do is stall. And if he's come to the conclusion that you are the culprit your anxiety to find out the facts might be misconstrued as guilt. I'd let well alone if I were you.'

'Easy to talk,' Sid sighed. Then he puckered his big face somewhat. 'Still, maybe you're right.'

Terry allowed a reasonable interval to pass whilst he mechanically put down entries in the film logbook. Then he turned.

'You'd better get the box tidied up, Sid. Billy's job for today, you know.'

'Fair enough.' Sid lumbered out willingly.

Terry waited until he could hear the heavy footsteps moving to and fro in the projection room above, then he began a search under the bench for the old and dusty film can which contained last season's carol. He found it presently, took the 150-length of film from the tin — and listened. Sid was still busy above, and likely to be for a little while.

Carefully Terry unwound the film until he came to the actual sound track. His recollection of it had been correct. At equal distances from each other, on the extreme outer edge, the track was punctured with holes. A measurement with a ruler satisfied him that the distance between each hole was about an eighth of an inch. He nodded to himself, put the film away again in the can, and then began to hunt around through the boxes of junk and spare parts until he found a suitable small-circumference gear wheel with a multitude of sharp teeth.

To find a long piece of steel with a thread at one end was not difficult. In the vice he bent the threaded section for a length of about an inch at right angles, until the finished rod looked like a letter 'L'. The base of the 'L' he pushed through the gear wheel's central hole, and with a bolt and washer fitted it into position. An

131

experiment on an old bit of film satisfied him that the device was perfect. With sufficient pressure the gear wheel left holes that almost touched each other.

Terry's urge now was to prepare the carol film for experiment, but he had to resist the temptation. Sid might come down at any moment: he must have no hint whatever. Terry decided that he could make his preparations at home during the dinner hour. For the moment he had done all he could — and if he was not to seem unusually busy down here he had better go up and join Sid. This he did, helping him in tidying the projection room and making preparations for the matinee.

At lunchtime Terry left a few minutes after Sid and took the Christmas carol film with him, small enough to fit into his pocket. He hurried through his lunch and then, with an excuse, he went up to his bedroom. Here, using the marble top of the old-fashioned washstand, he unrolled the film and in fifteen minutes had punctured the sprocket-side of the tracks from end to end with his homemade perforator.

So far, so good. He returned to the cinema ahead of Sid, put the carol film out of sight, and began normal duties. He would have to remain behind again tonight, and to build up to this he once more complained of machine trouble. Sid, completely unwary, again offered to stay — and once again Terry assured him there would be no necessity. As for Turner, he raised no objections.

The ensuing hours were leadenly monotonous for both of them — for Terry because he wanted to get on with his task; for Sid because hoped-for information did not come. The matinee passed, the tea hour, and the evening show — and once again Terry found himself repeating the actions of the night before. He told Turner he was again working on his machine. Turner did not question it; he had not the technical knowledge to do so.

Once more, as on the previous night, Terry waited until the building was deserted, then he went up into the false roof and lowered both the houselight over the tip-up seat, and its opposite neighbour. When he tried out his 'punctured' carol film he had to be sure that the houselight globes in a direct line with the screen speakers did not get the blast and crack in pieces.

This task completed he went to the washroom and found an empty tumbler over the lavatory bowl. He slipped it in his pocket and next went up to the projection room. In a moment or two he had laced up the carol film. He set the curtains sweeping back from the screen and for a moment gazed out onto the greyness lighted by a single high cleaning light.

He switched on the No. 1 projector but he did not use the arc. He did not need vision: only sound. Setting the sound-fader control at normal for the cinema he went out into the Circle and stood listening. Christmas bells were pealing out in all their glory, to the accompaniment of the 'First Noel'. That former high-pitched hum which had been present had gone. This fact could only mean that his multiplication of punctures had raised the pitch of the hum into the inaudible. Taking the tumbler out of his pocket he placed it on his palm. Then he held it over his head.

Nothing happened.

His eye on the clock — the film would take about seven minutes to run through — Terry climbed on the back seat of the Circle and raised the tumbler to the limit. Still nothing happened. Either he was not in a direct line with the supersonic vibration or else the idea wasn't feasible.

He looked at the glass portholes. They were not cracked, so evidently the supersonic wave wasn't affecting them either. His gaze moved round to the long-handled shovel standing in its clip amidst the fire-fighting hoses and sand buckets. He hurried over to it, pulled it forth, and then went up to the projection room with it.

Switching off the projector he re-threaded the film to the beginning, and by this time had fixed a rough platform on top of the long-handled fire shovel. With the projector again running he returned to the Circle, put the tumbler on top of the shovel platform and raised it high in the air. When it had reached a point about eight inches above the level of the portholes it suddenly splintered and bits of glass came raining down.

Terry dodged, grinning to himself. At that point, then, the supersonic vibration was in full blast, but missing all points below. He held the shovel's long handle in position for a while longer, estimating the height. It was about at the point where the houselights would be when hanging in the normal position.

'That's it!' Terry breathed. 'The point is, which will go first? The screws, or the glass of the globe? How am I to find that out?'

He put the shovel down, picked up every bit of tumbler glass he could find, and then returned upstairs to switch off the projector and think the business out. He had arrived at a ticklish problem, and it was a problem that couldn't be solved, either, without endangering the house-light globes. If one or both of them got broken in his endeavour to see if they *would* break, what then?

There was also another point. Was the supersonic vibration as powerful in *all directions* at that height? If so, its direction could be altered by tilting the speakers at the back of the screen . . .

Terry was commencing to realize he had still a long way to go. It was the recollection of a spare lower hemisphere globe in the winding room that set him off again. He got it, spent some time fixing up a rough device to hold the globe on top of his 'shovel extension', then with the projector once more running he returned to the Circle to experiment.

Everywhere he raised the test globe nothing happened, even though he knew the supersonic vibration must be beating against it. At last the film came to an end with a dull bump from the speakers. Terry lowered his aching arm.

'That settles it,' he muttered. 'This opal glass is too tough to be shattered by a supersonic wave. Being half an inch thick it isn't surprising. Okay, all I need now is a dress rehearsal.'

He went upstairs and stopped the racing machine; then he came back into the Circle and screwed and unscrewed the turnscrews of the globe, which would hang over the tip-up seat. Oil he did not dare to use, but after working on the screws for several minutes he was satisfied that they moved up and down with perfect ease in their threads. This done, he loosened all three until only their very tips were holding under the globe rim.

Returning to the false roof he hauled up both fixtures into place again — satisfied by now that the neighbour fixture would not be affected — and then he went into the staff room and gathered up a pile of dustsheets. These he bundled into a huge, bedlike mass round the tip-up seat beneath the hanging globe.

Going back to the projection room he rewound the carol film and started it up yet again. With keenly watching eyes he studied the globe slightly above his line of vision through the porthole. The film ran on for a minute and nothing happened. Two minutes — Three minutes. Terry found himself taut with expectancy, wondering if the whole idea was crazy anyway —

Then, without a sound, the lower white hemisphere suddenly fell out of its fitting and dropped in the centre of the mass of dust sheets. Terry switched off, his legs shaking.

It *could* be done — and, as he had calculated, the hemisphere's weight was such that it did not deviate from a straight line in its downward drop. Had Vera been sitting there . . .

'It works! It definitely works!' Terry kept telling himself, over and over again. 'And the time for the globe to cool to the point it is now means twenty minutes will have to elapse before the trouble starts. At that time we'll be starting the Travelogue on this machine of mine . . . Mmm, this has to be worked out.'

He glanced at his watch. It was half past eleven. Obviously the carol film could not be used to produce the supersonic wave. Only the Fitzpatrick Travelogue could be used for that. It was, as he knew, a new copy with a perfect sound track. He could quite easily put punctures down the side of the track from start to finish with his 'perforator', and the effect produced when the film was run could not fail to be the same as that produced by the experimental carol film because the punctures would have the same spacing and the film would be moving at the same speed.

'Tomorrow afternoon we shan't be using the Travelogue,' Terry went on, thinking. 'It's the kids' cowboy matinee. Tomorrow night will be the last run for the Travelogue. Then it will be stripped off and sent back to the renters. They'll examine it before sending it off to another cinema and those perforations will then be found . . . '

Therein lay the snag. The film renters would have a record of the film as *perfect* when sent to the Cosy Cinema, and *damaged* when received back. Even though the minute holes would not interfere with the recording itself — as heard in the cinema — the film would no longer be classed as good copy. Attention would be drawn to the perforations. Then matters would work round to a difficult situation.

'That's a risk I daren't take,' Terry told himself, looking at his machine absently. 'There's only one other way — deliberately ruin the sound track! Scratch it to blazes so the film can never be run again. That will mean the renters' attention will be confined to the scratching, and the perforations, if noticed at all, will not even be mentioned. There'll be hell to play, of course, and Turner will have to pay for the damage, but that can't be helped . . . Yes, that's the idea! I can say that the machine I've been working on still isn't right and that that is what must have caused the damage. Perfect! Ruin the film after we've run it for the last time. In that condition the film will be scrapped by the renters. They'll get rid of the evidence, and not be aware of it!'

The problem of how to deliberately ruin the film did not trouble him for a moment. All he had to do, when standing beside his machine, was to let the point of a needle scratch the track severely as the film ran out below the sound gate. If the film were ever run again it would be one mass of explosions, bangs, and interference.

Terry's mind was made up, but a rehearsal was still called for.

He went into the winding room and,

because Sid had done his job properly during the day the Travelogue film was duly wound back to the start. That meant it would not be examined again before being run at the show. Putting it on the winder, Terry wound it back to the finish, using his perforator all along the track on the sprocket side — the side that would be nearest to him when the film ran. This done, he wound the film back to start, took it up to his projector and laced it through, laying the carol film on one side for the moment.

His next actions took him half an hour. He had to replace the hemisphere globe and haul it back into the ceiling. Then he went back to his machine, struck up the arc, and ran the Travelogue as he would at a normal performance. It had reached the halfway point, giving a view of a Technicolor bay on the screen, when the thing happened. The globe dropped, once again into the dust sheets.

Terry switched off and calculated the time. At exactly five minutes to eight the following evening the globe would drop!

In another couple of hours everything

was ready. He had put the precariously screwed globe back in position, the turn-screw tips on the very edge of the glass rim. The dust sheets were back in the staff room, and curtains were redrawn across the screen, and the carol film burned to ashes and scattered to the night wind from the fire escape.

The only thing Terry could not replace was the tumbler from the washroom, but he resolved to bring one next morning. The Travelogue was rewound and in the bin ready for the actual performance. As far as Terry was concerned Vera Holdsworth's fate was settled, and his own position unassailable.

6

Globe of death

At nine the following morning Terry arrived at the cinema looking hollow-eyed and strained about the mouth. He explained away his condition as being the beginning of a cold and spent most of the morning filled with a deep foreboding. Whilst he had been working out the problem in supersonics he had been happy: he had hardly glimpsed the underlying fiendishness of the motive for it all. Now he'd had the opportunity for more or less sober reflection he was frightened. Several times during the morning, as he worked beside Sid, he was more than once tempted to say it was time the houselights had a clean, and thereby get the chance to put the globe back to normal.

No; things were too far advanced for that. The Travelogue film was perforated and ready. There was no reasonable excuse he could invent for leaving it out of the programme that night. The thing had to go on, and with this realization he steeled himself again.

It *had* to be done. It was the only way to escape imprisonment, and anyway Vera was not the sort of girl whose being alive did anybody any good — except herself.

It was after the children's matinee, as Terry went across to the café for a cup of tea, that Helen Prescott caught up with him. He turned in surprise in the cafe doorway.

'Why, Helen!'

'Right!' she agreed, with a bright smile. 'Do you mind? I eat, you know, same as other people.'

Terry held the door open for her and they went across together to a corner table. Terry gave the order for both of them and then gave a questioning glance.

'What's the idea, Helen? Given up going home for tea?'

'Not altogether, only my folks and sis are out a good deal, and there's nothing I dislike more than having to eat alone.'

Terry laughed a little. 'It's a wonder the

boss doesn't invite you to tea with him!'

'That,' Helen said, her pretty face serious, 'is why I'm here with you.'

'Why me? I don't get it.'

'It's simple enough. He's aching to take me out to tea: he even said so. But somehow I — Well, it just doesn't seem right. I'm only an employee after all, and he *is* the boss.'

'Am I supposed to feel flattered?' Terry asked, and he had to wait for the tea to be laid out before he got an answer.

'Maybe it's a strange admission for me to make,' Helen said pensively, 'but I really would give anything to know you better, Terry. You're a decent chap to work with, and a good looker. I just can't understand why I don't seem to . . . to warm up to you, as it were.'

'Easily explained,' Terry shrugged. 'The boss is worth a few thousands and has some standing. I'm miles below him. That's why you don't warm up to me. No girl in her right senses would.'

'Don't make any mistake! Not every girl is out for what she can get! We're not all like Vera Holdsworth, for instance.'

Terry said nothing. He was watching Helen's slender hands as she poured out the tea.

'You've had a pretty bad experience with her,' she went on. 'Naturally it has influenced your judgment with all girls — which isn't exactly fair to either side. You surely don't think I'm like *her*, do you?'

'You couldn't be,' Terry said. 'But I don't see why you have to tag along with me.'

'Look, Terry, didn't you say yourself we ought to make a go of it together?'

'Yes . . . But that was before I realized just how much the boss means to you.'

Helen handed the teacup across. 'You've got it all wrong, Terry. He doesn't mean anything to me: it's the other way round. But since he is the boss I have to take care what I do. Can't bluntly refuse his advances, you know.'

'If your affection is mainly for me you wouldn't have any qualms about telling him to go to blazes,' Terry said frankly.

'First I want to find out if it really *is* affection I have for you,' Helen said slowly, her eyes fixed on him. 'You seem to have most of the things a girl looks for in a man, but — There's a barrier somehow,' she added frowning. 'I don't know what it can be, either.'

'Sounds crazy to me,' Terry growled.

'I'm sensitive to people,' Helen explained. 'I sort of know what they're really like. I even find it annoying sometimes, when I want to like a person and yet just can't because an inner sense keeps telling me to keep away. As far as the boss is concerned, I know that if I went overboard for him I'd end up as quite an influential wife, and he'd probably be a quiet, dead-level husband, never getting excited, and because of that a plain bore. With you there's more fire and purpose — more imagination. But there's also something else which I can't get at.'

Terry sighed and then went on with his tea. The girl's next words gave him a shock.

'You've something on your mind, Terry. Won't you tell me what it is? I'll help if I can.'

For a long moment he looked at her as though she were a total stranger. He even felt half afraid of her.

'Friends should help, shouldn't they?' she insisted. 'And there is certainly something worrying you. What is it? I can't get at it.'

'Do you have to?' Terry demanded roughly. 'I've nothing on my mind except the burglary. I'm worried about that because I don't know who'll be nailed for it. It might even be me.'

'You've mentioned that before. But you didn't do it, did you?'

'Do it?' Terry gave an indignant glare. 'Of course not!'

'Then what is it? And anyway, I don't think it's just that that's bothering you. You're not the kind of chap to worry over such a thing. It's something else. Perhaps domestic or maybe money troubles . . . ' Helen's hand suddenly reached across the table and gripped Terry's firmly. 'Terry, I'm in earnest. I do want to know you better, and I'd do anything if I could.'

'Of course.' Terry smiled. 'It's nothing, Helen. And the sooner you stop psycho-analyzing me and go back to the boss, the better.'

The outburst only made Helen smile. Quite undisturbed, she went on with her tea.

'You gave yourself away, you know,' she said presently. 'There must be something on your mind or you wouldn't have flared up like that! Don't tell me if you don't want to: I don't want to pry.'

Helen meditated for a long time as she ate, her eyes on Terry's morose face and averted eyes. Finally she sighed.

'All right, if that's how you feel about it. In the meantime, if your troubles get you down, don't forget that I'm your friend.'

She did not press matters any further. When she and Terry left the café together it was she who did most of the talking. Terry for his part was measuring the minutes. At 7-55 that globe would drop. He found it enormously difficult to sound natural as he spoke, and he hoped that Helen would not notice his preoccupation. But she did. Once or twice he found her eyes fixed on him in complete wonder . . .

He was glad to part from her when

they reached the cinema. Though he had not admitted a single fact that might be construed as a clue to his intentions, he felt just as though he had told everything, that Helen knew every detail. Naturally, she did not, but that did not prevent her carrying her wonderment with her as she entered the staff dressing room to change into her uniform.

For Terry, everything was mechanical. Sid was mainly silent and moody. Billy, as usual, was an infernal nuisance with his piercing whistling and decidedly doubtful jokes.

At 7-50 to the minute Terry dimmed the houselights and gazed out onto to the Circle as he did so. Being Saturday night the house was packed to the last seat. He had banked on that. It meant that Vera would not have so much running about to do once the first ten minutes had passed. Patrons rarely arrived very late at the Cosy; it was a family cinema to which everybody contrived to arrive on time.

At the moment Vera was busy with her torch, showing a man and woman into Row C. Then the lights expired and the news began. It finished. Sid ran the comedy. His big, heavy face was quite expressionless as he stared through the porthole at the screen.

At this distance it looked like a postage stamp. Billy came in and brought the Travelogue spool. Terry took it from him.

'I'll lace up,' Terry said briefly. 'Get the news stripped off, Billy.'

'Okay.'

The door slammed on its springs. Terry found himself sweating. He put the spool in the top fireproof box with a noisy rattle, whirled the spool round to free a length of leader film for lacing.

'Fitz,' he said curtly.

'Fitz — check,' Sid acknowledged.

Terry's hands were shaking as he laced up. He even wondered once if he had a dream or something. Had he really prepared the film the night before? Yes. He had prepared it all right. When he ran the film down to the censor's certificate he could see the title just above it, and the start of the sound track. The punctures were there all right.

He finished lacing, re-carboned the arc,

then leaned on the projector to watch the comedy. It did not strike him as at all funny . . . Gently, from the lining of his waistcoat, he pulled out a sharp needle and concealed it in his palm.

7-45 . . . At 7-50 Sid nodded and glanced round from his machine.

'Nearly off, Terry. Strike up.'

Terry hesitated; then he set his mouth, and struck the arc. The carbons sizzled and flared. White light gushed blindingly on the white coat inside of the arc chimney. He looked down at the Circle.

Vera was there, seated on the tip-up, just as he had expected.

'Motor!' Sid called, and Terry snapped the motor switch.

His projector gathered speed and opened up as Sid's machine closed down. The certificate flashed through briefly and the musical accompaniment to James Fitzpatrick's Travelogue began. On the screen was the familiar Technicolour face of the world with rays radiating from it.

Tense, completely silent, Terry stood by his machine. The point of the needle he was holding was relentlessly scraping the film track below the sound gate. The fact that he was doing this could not be detected. His body hid his hand as it lay in the sound gate box.

It was eight minutes to eight. In three minutes, according to plan, Vera would be in —

'Huh!' Sid exclaimed, peering through his own porthole into the Circle. 'Wonder what happened to Vera?'

'Eh?' Terry gave a start. He stood up straight. He had been looking at the screen and clock. He had to peer downwards to see the tip-up. There was somebody seated there, quite distinct in the reflected glow from the picture beam.

'That's Helen Prescott,' Sid said, taking the spool out of the bottom of his machine. 'Not often Vera gets called away — Say, I wonder if something has developed about the burglary? She may be down with the boss . . . '

Helen! There! And only one minute to go!

Terry did not even stop to think. He made a wild grab at the speeding film as it came out of the box to the top sprocket.

The wrench snapped the film in two. There was a dull crack from the monitor-speaker and a blaze of white light on the screen. Then Terry slammed down the shutter, switched off, and swore.

'What the hell?' Sid stared at him. 'What's up? A break? I'll skin Billy's hide when I get him. Saturday night, too!' He raced round to Terry's side. 'Hang it man, why don't you lace up . . . ?'

Terry shook his head stupidly. His face was white. He did not speak or think. Then he looked at the first and second finger of his right hand. They were streaming with blood. In his dive at the film his fingers had been carried through the sharp teeth of the sprocket.

'Okay,' Sid said curtly, who had seen and experienced such mishaps before. 'I'll lace. You can't.'

'But look — '

'Out of the way, man!' Sid roared. 'The show's being held up! There — listen!'

The buzzer, actuated from the stalls, was sounding sharply. Evidently Mark Turner was getting impatient. If the audience was indulging in any of its inane

155

clapping and foot stamping it could not be heard up here through the immensely thick walls.

Dazed, wrapping a handkerchief round his lacerated fingers, Terry watched as with experienced hands Sid re-laced the machine at top speed and then started it up again.

'Okay, I'll run it,' he said.

Terry shook his head stubbornly. He almost elbowed Sid out of the way and took over the machine again. He stared into Circle — then drew a deep breath. Helen was gone and Vera was back on the tip-up seat. His left hand was shaking as he put the needle point back on the speeding film and held it there. Through the handkerchief on his right hand blood was seeping through.

The clock said three minutes to eight. Two minutes lost. Terry's eyes strayed to the faintly visible globe. It was still intact.

Two minutes to eight, and James Fitzpatrick was getting well into his stride — Then Terry saw it happen. Silently the lower hemisphere of the globe dropped downwards and vanished.

Nothing. He could not hear a sound through the walls, but he was shaking so violently he could hardly stand. Sid noticed his distress and assumed it was because of his injured hand.

'Say,' he remarked, as Billy handed in the first two reels of the feature, 'you ought to get down to the first aid kit with that hand, Terry. You've chewed it to hell and you're as white as a ghost.'

Terry could not answer: his mouth was too dry. He jumped at a sudden saving buzzing on the interphone. With his bandaged hand he reached out and picked the phone up.

'Yes?' His voice was husky. 'Terry speaking.'

'Kill the show, Terry.' It was Turner's voice, shaken for once. 'Been a bad accident. Put the lights up.'

'Accident?' Terry repeated, and he was so worked up he did not need to act to sound horrified. 'What's happened?'

'A houselight globe's come down — hit Miss Holdsworth. Hurry up with the lights, man!'

Terry closed the shutter of the

projector and cut off the hall sound. He put up the houselights and left his machine running, with his hand guiding the ruinous needle. With Sid he looked out onto the Circle.

'What's happened?' Sid demanded, puzzled. 'I can't see anything for people.'

Terry said nothing. The audience was moving — a shifting throng about the top of the steps and the tip-up seat. In other directions people were standing up and craning their necks. The screen was a blank oblong, hazed by the blue of tobacco smoke.

'What did the boss say?' Sid insisted. 'Somebody passed out?'

With a rattle and snap the Travelogue came to an end and its leader length clattered into the bottom spool-box. Terry switched off and jabbed the needle in the hem of his waistcoat. When the noisy machine had whined into quietness the silence seemed appalling.

'What *happened?*' Sid repeated, mystified. 'Is — Say!'

His voice changed. 'There's a house-light underglobe missing up there! Has it

— By God, don't tell me it dropped on
. . . on Vera!'

'Yes. That's what the boss said.' Terry
spoke quietly, and with considerable
effort. 'I didn't dare tell you, knowing
how fond you are of Vera — '

Sid swung and dived across the
projection room. Terry whirled him back
as he reached the spring door.

'Wait a minute!' Terry snapped. 'Where
are you going?'

'To see what's happened to Vera, of
course! She's my girl, isn't she?'

'There's nothing you can do, and your
job's up here. Get a hold on yourself,
man!'

Terry looked through the porthole and
then turned away. He had caught one
glimpse of what had really happened as,
for a moment, the people surged apart.
Chunks of white globe lay in various
directions. Vera was stretched full length
on the floor, her head invisible with the
amount of rough wadding and bandages
which had been wrapped about it.

For a moment Terry thought he was
going to faint.

It seemed an interminable time to him before uniformed ambulance men appeared with a stretcher and the motionless girl was down the steps and out of view. Terry waited with arid lips. Harry, the doorman, appeared and began brushing up the chunks of opal glass.

He had just finished when the interphone buzzed.

'Carry on,' Turner said, in possession of himself again. 'Leave out the interval and go right on with the feature.'

'Yes, sir,' Terry said mechanically, and glanced at Sid. 'Get started, Sid. No interval.'

Obviously stupefied, Sid switched on his machine and the feature began. Slowly Terry dimmed the houselights to extinction.

'How can they go on with this show when Vera's hurt — maybe even dead?' Sid demanded in sudden anger. 'It's — inhuman!'

'A show's a show, Vera or no Vera,' Terry replied. 'The people have paid their money and they have to be given an entertainment. You carry on: I'll go down and see what really happened.'

Terry was quite calm again now. The thing was done and he even felt less guilty than he had expected because he had made an effort to stop the crime. Sid had insisted on re-threading the film: that had left no other course than to go straight on.

Terry called for Billy and had him do the lacing; then Terry hurried down to the winding room and unwrapped the blood-spattered handkerchief from about his fingers. They were badly chopped up — no doubt about it — with sprocket teeth marks across them. Set-faced, Terry bound them up with lint and bandaging after washing them under the cold water tap, then he went downstairs to find Mark Turner.

Turner was in his office, immaculate as usual in his 'monkey suit', but his face showed he was considerably shaken.

'What happened, sir?' Terry asked, and his strained voice sounded like genuine anxiety.

'Horrible business, Terry.' Turner pressed finger and thumb to his eyes and gave his head a little shake. 'I've heard of such things happening in other theatres and cinemas, but that it should have to happen *here!* That poor girl . . . '

'I — I noticed a houselight underglobe had gone,' Terry said. 'Then I saw Vera with her head wrapped up lying on the floor — '

'She lived for a few minutes,' Turner said, in a colourless voice, staring before him. 'It's the worst accident I've ever seen. I've sent Harry to advise her parents, and the police will be here soon. The coroner will be advised, of course. The police will want to examine the lamp when the show's over.'

Terry nodded slowly. This was no more than he had expected.

'I'll have to ring my solicitor and find out if I'm liable,' Turner added. 'Or it may come under her union. Soon find out. And you and Sid must stay after the show. You two are responsible for the houselights — cleaning them and so on. The police will want to ask you a question or two.'

'Yes, of course,' Terry agreed. 'Frankly,

sir, I just don't understand it. Seems no reason why a globe should fall like that.'

Turner shrugged. 'Just one of those things, I suppose. I understand it caught Miss Holdsworth at an angle, with such force that the glass splintered. She was terribly hurt . . . That's all for now, Terry. Try and keep your mind on the show — What's happened to your hand?' Turner broke off, staring at it.

'This?' Terry looked at his bandaged fingers. 'Oh, nothing. The Travelogue film broke, as you know. I was using too many fingers in trying to save it and I got mixed up with the gears.'

'Serious?' Turner questioned, having the feeling that fresh liabilities were piling up.

'No, sir; it'll be all right. This must be one of those nights. It isn't the first time I've done it, anyway.' Terry lowered his hand and shook his head gloomily. 'I just can't get over this awful business. Come to think of it, had it been a minute or two sooner Helen might have got it.'

Vague surprise kindled in Turner's ayes. 'Helen Prescott, you mean? Mmm — yes.

She relieved Vera for a moment or two while Vera came down here for a new torch battery.'

So that had been it! Nothing more than that.

'How did you notice?' Turner asked.

'About Helen?' Terry hesitated briefly and then gave a shrug. 'I didn't: it was Sid. He's crazy about Vera, you know — or I should say *was*. He soon noticed that she'd gone from the tip-up. I think her sitting down there sort of gave him moral support, or something.'

Turner nodded absently and then turned back to his desk. Terry went out silently and closed the door . . . And by the time he returned upstairs he had got completely over his jitters. Vera was dead! There was no longer a witness who could prove he was a thief, and certainly there was no clue to show he was a murderer as well. The police wouldn't find a thing to pin on him.

Entering the winding-room, he made sure that Billy had duly stripped off the Travelogue film and that it was safely in its transit case. Naturally, Billy would have repaired the break that had been made. At midnight the transport man would come and take the film away with the rest of the finished programme. Then the renters would write and complain of damage. Terry knew to the last detail just how things would work out.

He went up into the projection room and for the rest of the show had his time fully occupied in dealing with Sid. For Sid, to the strain of thinking that he might at any moment be arrested for a theft he had not committed, there was now added the crushing blow of bereavement. He had really been fond of Vera; there was no doubt about that now.

First he raved, then he wept — but he kept at his job through a sheer dogged sense of duty. Young Billy got the facts in bits and pieces, and the knowledge that Vera had been killed left him round-eyed and quiet — for a time. Then towards the end of the evening he was whistling again, a sure sign that he had absorbed the shock and cast it on one side as of no consequence.

As instructed, Terry and Sid stayed

behind after the show. They hung about the foyer long after the rest of the staff had gone, whilst the police — under the direction of Superintendent Standish once again — had the offending house-light lowered and examined. During this task Turner was upstairs in the Circle, too, then at length he, the Superintendent, and a detective-sergeant, came down into the foyer.

Terry was perfectly calm. Sid was the more worked up. He had not Terry's frigid mastery of his emotions.

'Evening, chief,' the superintendent said. 'I don't have to tell you what happened, I just want a few particulars for the inquest . . . The houselights are your responsibility, I understand?'

'That's right,' Terry agreed — and thus began a routine of questions, which he answered truthfully, with verification from Sid when necessary.

'Thanks very much,' the Super said finally, and turned to the manager. 'We'll leave the houselight where it is for tonight, lowered to the floor of the Circle. First thing tomorrow I'll have experts over from Farnington to give their opinion. I'm not an expert — just a police official. You're open Sundays, aren't you?'

'Morning and evening,' Turner answered. 'No matinee. We'll be here as usual in the morning.'

'Good. You've advised the girl's parents?'

'Yes, and informed her union secretary. The liability is theirs, not mine.'

In a few moments the Super and detective-sergeant took their departure. Terry watched the foyer doors close on them, and then he glanced at Turner. 'How do you suppose I'll get on, sir?' he asked. 'Do you think the police can prove negligence on my part, or Sid's?'

'I don't see for a single moment how they can. I don't know what made the globe fall, but the experts will no doubt soon find out. Certainly I don't see how you two can be accused of anything.'

'To be hoped not,' Sid muttered. 'It'd be manslaughter.'

'Nothing to worry over, I'm sure,' Turner said. 'Well, goodnight boys, and thanks for staying.'

'Oh, Mr. Turner . . . ' Sid spoke as though he had suddenly come to a decision. 'I've been meaning to ask you . . . '

'Yes?' Turner waited.

'About the burglary,' Sid went on impulsively. 'How far have the police got? I keep having this horrible feeling that they suspect me, though I'm innocent, God knows. There's no other way I can interpret their silence. I can't stand the thought of that possibility on top of knowing that Vera's dead. What has happened?'

Turner shrugged. 'Frankly, I don't know. These things take a good deal of time, you know, particularly when there isn't much to go on. The police told me they're going to continue their inquiry, and I suppose that's what they are doing. That's all I know, I'm afraid.'

Turner turned back into his office and Sid and Terry glanced at each other. Then without speaking they turned away.

★　★　★

For Terry the night was tortured by hideous nightmares. Time and again he saw that globe dropping in the dim reflection cast by the projector beam. The throbbing of his bandaged hand made him live over again that frantic moment when he had snatched at the film and broken it rather than have the globe fall on Helen Prescott.

Why had he done that? He asked himself the question over and over. He wanted to love Helen, but how could he if Mark Turner had got there before him? He did love her. Deep down in his heart he knew he did, and that was the main reason why he had risked so much in stopping the show.

For it *had* been a risk. As time went on, Sid, morose at the death of Vera, might get to thinking. He knew the Fitzpatrick Travelogue film was a good copy — not a joint in it anywhere. So why had it broken, as it apparently had? Terry realized he must be ready for this problem when it arose.

What else was there? Terry recapitulated silently to himself.

Apparently he had taken care of everything. Nothing had been left undone, and he had cleared up all the remains of his tests. Glass shreds, dust sheets, tumbler — Hell, that tumbler! He had not put another one in the washroom; forgotten all about it. Well, no harm done. He could easily say it had got broken and that would not raise any question he couldn't deal with.

There was no turning back now. Whatever happened, he had got to lie himself out of every difficulty in which he found himself.

The one person to be wary of was Sid. Plodding, technically brilliant, and bereft of all interest in living at the moment because of the death of the girl he had loved. If he ever got the vaguest hint there would be no stopping him. He would plough on like a juggernaut until he had every detail. And then . . .

The following morning the two experts would arrive to examine the houselight. Terry resolved to keep out of their way as much as possible — which was exactly what he did — or almost. He had to go into the Circle as it happened, and sit through the rehearsal programme for Sunday and the ensuing three days. Out of the corner of his eye he noticed that they examined the fitting thoroughly, and the glass pieces which Harry had put aside in a separate box. Then the two men went up into the false roof and stayed there for a considerable time. After which Terry saw no more of them.

The matter did not come up again until the following — Monday — morning when the inquest was held, and Terry and Sid — despite it being Sid's normal day off — found themselves amongst the witnesses along with Turner and three members of the audience who had seen the globe fall.

The more the Coroner had to say the more Terry realized how far away he was from being suspected. It was the evidence of one of the experts that satisfied him that he had conceived and executed a perfect crime.

' . . . and, Mr. Gray,' the Coroner said, addressing the expert, 'you are perfectly satisfied that every normal precaution was taken in regard to that particular houselight in question?'

'Perfectly,' Gray agreed. 'My colleague and I have formed the only possible theory. The metal of the lamp fixture must, of course, have contracted after the heat of the bulb. The screws holding the underglobe were never made very tight — to which fact the chief projectionist has testified — since the expansion of the glass underneath might cause the glass to crack and fall. I believe there was a draught blowing on the lamp fixture from one of the wall ventilators. It is possible that the cool stream of air caused the metal to contract slightly more than usual so that as it tightened up the glass lip of the globe was bitten into by the screws. Consequently the glass lip broke and came down.'

'In other words,' the Coroner said, 'the screws were a trifle too tight and the unhappy chance of cold air caused an extreme instead of a normal contraction?'

'That I believe to be the case, sir. It is quite possible, as it has happened before in theatres and cinemas. Because of that chance most cinemas and theatres have done away with the screw-type globe and instead are using fixtures imbedded in the ceiling — or else concealed lighting, which is safest of all.'

There seemed to be nothing more to be said. A verdict of 'Death from Misadventure' was returned and Turner was advised to replace the clumsy old houselights with something less heavy and more modern, to which he promptly agreed. After that, beyond condolences to the relatives and friends of the deceased, the matter was done with . . .

7

Sid investigates

Terry felt as though tons of weight had been lifted from his mind. He had got away with the perfect burglary and the perfect murder. Only some slip on his part could ever bring the truth to light and he was firmly determined that no such slip should ever take place.

He went back to the cinema and Sid accompanied him — not to work, for he intended using what remained of his day off, but to talk.

When they returned to the cinema they found Turner had already arrived ahead of them in his car. He promptly called Terry into his office.

'I don't care what you spend, Terry,' he said, 'but get new fixtures ordered and put them up the moment they arrive.'

'I'll see right away what we want, sir,' Terry promised. 'Then I'll let you have the order to sign and dispatch.'

'Right — Oh, one minute. There's one other thing. The staff is getting up a subscription for a wreath for Miss Holdsworth. The funeral will be on Wednesday. Naturally you'll want to subscribe?'

'Of course . . . ' Terry fished out a handful of coins and put them on the desk. 'All the change I have sir, I'm afraid.'

'Entirely up to you. Send in Sid, will you?'

Terry nodded and left the office. He waited until Sid came into view again after his brief discourse with Turner.

'How much did you contribute to the wreath?' Sid asked gloomily.

'Four shillings. All the change I've got.'

'Four shillings! You don't rate Vera's wreath very highly, do you?'

'Matter of fact, no,' Terry shrugged. 'You know how I felt about her. No reason why I should start feeling affectionate towards her memory.'

Sid did not say anything. He and Terry came to the halfway point of the Circle stairway. They turned in at their own private doorway.

'I *still* don't see how it happened,' Sid muttered, half to himself.

'It was made plain enough at the inquest, wasn't it? The experts explained exactly what took place.'

'You mean they *tried* to explain. It didn't sound at all convincing to me. They had to say something, so they said that.'

At noon, Sid departed to take the rest of the day off — and Terry, to his surprise, found Helen waiting for him at the front of the building. It was quite unexpected, and he gave her a questioning look.

'I've been doing a lot of thinking,' she explained. 'As we walk along I thought I could tell you about it.'

'By all means,' Terry agreed, taking her arm.

'You seem remarkably cheerful all of a sudden.' Helen gave him a quick glance. 'I haven't seen you in such a good humour for many a long day. What's happened? And after the inquest, too!'

176

Terry looked at her seriously. She gave a little sigh.

'All right, it wasn't funny,' she confessed. 'Bad taste on my part . . . Honest, though, I can't work up any deep sorrow for Vera. I never liked her, as you know.'

'That I'm cheerful has nothing to do with, her, or the inquest,' Terry said, then he corrected himself. 'Well, maybe the inquest has something to do with it. The experts proved that Sid and I are quite guiltless in the matter, so naturally it's a load off my mind.'

Helen looked vaguely mystified. 'What else did you expect, anyway? You surely didn't think anybody did have anything to do with the accident, did you?'

'No, but they might have found a way to prove negligence, and that might have meant manslaughter . . . Oh, let's forget it! What is it you've been thinking about?'

'It concerns you and I. I've spent some time wondering, and maybe we could make something of our lives if we teamed up.'

Terry's eyes brightened, though his voice was hesitant.

'Well, that's fine! Something I've always dreamed about . . . One thing you must try and do, though — change your day off to Tuesday, same as mine.'

'I can try.' Helen sounded none too hopeful. 'The only snag is that the boss knows it's your day and he may refuse to let me have mine then for that very reason. It isn't usual to give a rival every advantage, is it?'

'Definitely not.' Terry gave a sigh. 'Try, anyway.'

'You bet I will. I'll try with everything I've got!'

Terry had arrived at the conclusion that this was his lucky day. The inquest had proved him innocent, and the girl he really loved was at last coming round to his way of thinking. As they talked and wandered along he mentally made plans to press home his advantage. Helen was young, pretty, and loyal. A girl of her type, after the Vera Holdsworth variety, might make all the difference to one's outlook, Terry decided . . .

The following day, Tuesday — Terry's day off — Sid was automatically in charge

178

of the projection department. He did not take it as an opportunity to be officious: in fact he would hardly have known how. Swank and authority were two traits that didn't exist in his downright, earthy nature.

When he arrived in the morning he gave a few orders to Billy, made sure everything was ready for the matinee, and then he went into the Circle to carry on with the task of erecting the still-frame on the Circle wall. He was still feeling the hurt of Vera's death, but perhaps not quite so keenly. By very slow degrees it was dawning on him that life goes on just the same for other people even when one is removed.

'Vera was somehow different, though,' he muttered, putting the ladder in place against the wall. 'Not many other girls I'd trust. They fly off the handle for no reason at all — and one half of 'em don't mean what they say. Whole world's crazy,' he added, half aloud.

'You can say that again!' observed the doorman, and he rose unexpectedly from behind a seat he was repairing.

179

Sid lighted a Turkish cigarette and looked at him.

'So that's it? Sneaking up on me, eh?'

Harry only grinned. He held up a small, curved sliver of glass, which caught the cleaning light from the ceiling.

'Pretty, isn't it?' he asked sourly. 'Nearly cut me blasted 'and on it. Lucky one of the patrons didn't get it in 'im, or there'd 'ave been 'ell to pop.'

Sid looked at it and frowned. 'Where did it come from, anyway? Looks like part of a bulb, but I don't see how it can be.'

He came over and examined the fragment carefully. The doorman scratched his chin thoughtfully.

'It ain't part of a bulb, Sid,' he decided. 'It's part of a tumbler. Look, one edge is blunt. The part y' shove in yer mouth . . . '

'Mmmm, so it is.' Sid's eyes were faintly perplexed. 'Any more bits lying about?'

'I 'aven't seen any — an' I wouldn't 'ave found this except for two reasons. Repairin' this seat for one thing — and them lasses 'aven't cleaned up as well as they should. Not as I blame 'em, mind you — rottin' their young lives away in this dump — '

'Dump my foot!' Sid objected. 'They get good wages and the union looks after their hours. They might do a damned sight worse.'

'All right, all right, don't get excited. I ain't a girl, and I ain't young any more. I've got my *own* ideas about this place, I 'ave.'

Muttering to himself, the doorman went along the row of seats with the glass sliver in his hand. Sid watched him go, trying to imagine how a piece of glass had ever got on the floor of the Circle in the first place.

'Must be from lemonade refreshments,' he muttered at last. 'Somebody bust a glass, picked the bits up, but missed that chunk. Quite possible . . . '

It had been some time, though, since lemonade had been served, and even then it was usually in bottles with a straw. But there *must* have been a glass at some period, and the odd piece had been overlooked by the none-too-industrious girls.

Sid gave up thinking about the business and mounted the ladder to the top of the still-case. Smoking vigorously, he felt in his pocket for the screwdriver — then in mid-action he paused. Utter perplexity settled on his face.

'By all that's weird!' he exclaimed.

He could not quite understand what he saw. When he had left the still-case on the previous occasion he had placed two large, flat-headed screws on top of the case ready for the next operation this morning. Their heads had been resting on the polished wood, their points in the air. Beyond the slightest shadow of doubt Sid knew he had placed those screws at the right hand end of the case top. He was always methodical in such matters.

Now they were at the *left* hand and — and widely separated.

Nor, puzzling though it was, was this all. On the surface of the polished wood a good deal of light dust had settled, and in the midst of it lay a distinct trail, zigzagging, where the screws had made their journey from one end of the wood top to the other, until the quarter-inch beading had prevented them from falling off altogether. Finally — quite the most surprising thing Sid had ever seen — the dust was not so smooth as it ought to be. It was patterned, somehow. It even had a queer beauty of circles, whirligigs, and crescents, all perfectly formed. In places it banked up into tiny ridges, each ridge forming a remarkable design.

'What the devil?' Sid asked himself, utterly perplexed. 'How did *this* happen? Nobody could get up here without ladders — and even if they could they wouldn't want to move the screws and shift the dust into fancy shapes. I'll be hanged if anybody *could* draw designs as perfectly as these are drawn, outside of a professional artist.'

And there were certainly no artists in the Cosy Cinema.

For a long time Sid was stumped. The designs in the dust reminded him of something he had seen somewhere. A film it had been. Years ago. For the life of him he could not at the moment recall the connection.

'Beyond me,' he growled at length, and

with a shrug he went on with his job for a while, using the two screws to secure the frame more solidly to the plugs already driven in the wall. Nevertheless, as he worked, the problem bothered him. Yes, he *had* seen a design like this somewhere.

When he had finished his work — and the puzzle in the dust intrigued him so much that he did his job mechanically and without any special interest — he returned to the winding room and sat down on a transit case to think. Billy gave him a curious glance.

'What's the matter, apeman? Belly ache?'

Sid glared. 'Of course not, you little twerp! And stop calling me 'apeman' or I'll pin your ears back! If you must know, I'm thinking.'

Billy grinned and went on with his film winding. 'Mind something doesn't bust. You're not used to it, remember.'

Ordinarily, for this piece of impudence, Billy would have found himself dumped in the fire bucket — but this time nothing happened. And the fact profoundly surprised him. He stole a glance at Sid's faraway expression, and wondered.

'Look,' Sid said abruptly, 'I'm trying to remember something, and I don't seem to be doing too well. I've seen a film somewhere that was all designs and whirligigs. I seem to think it had prehistoric monsters in it, too.'

'Eh?' Billy gasped, staring. 'What did you have for breakfast?'

'I'm not kidding. Honest!' There was dogged earnestness in Sid's face. 'There *was* such a film. I saw it. In fact we ran it here when I was a rewind boy. It was an old film we were reviving.'

Billy's expression changed. He was proud of his cinematic knowledge.

'How long ago?'

'Oh, a long time. Maybe seven or eight years.'

'I'd be about ten then.' Billy did not seem to think that this was any deterrent. He had been going to pictures ever since he could remember. 'Prehistoric monsters?' he repeated. 'How about 'King Kong'?'

'No. It wasn't 'King Kong'.'

'Well, then, what about the 'Lost

World'? That had a whole flock of prehistoric monsters in it.'

Sid shook his head. 'It wasn't the 'Lost World' either. And there were no whirligigs in those two pictures — the film I saw was in colour. I remember that much.'

There was a long silence, then Billy's eyes brightened.

'*I* know! Would it be Walt Disney's 'Fantasia'? That was all colours, whirligigs, and monsters. Smashing film, even if I didn't know what it was all about. I remember that I — '

'That's it!' Sid sat up, an alert look on his face. 'Fantasia'! There were two reels all about an excursion into the film's sound track. I remember it fascinated me. The sound track was invited to come out from the side of the film and talk to the audience.'

'Right enough,' Billy agreed promptly. 'I remember that bit, too. Crafty bit of work. The track didn't speak. It just made itself up into all sorts of designs, and each design was meant to be a word — '

'That is partly right,' Sid assented

slowly, his technical mind sorting things out. 'What really happened was that the sound track was photographed down the middle of the film as well as being at the side in the ordinary way. Every note or sibilance of the voice makes a design in the track, and every one is different. They look like flowers, trees, branches, zigzags of all sorts. Yes . . . that's right.'

The faraway look returned to Sid's face. Billy's expression was puzzled, but interested.

'Might I say so what?' he asked presently.

'Never mind — just a thought I got.' Sid was still pondering. 'Just get on with your job, you little loafer. I'll go and carbon up ready for this afternoon.'

'I've done that already.'

'You have? Oh well, I'll go up into the box anyway.'

Sid left the winding room with his heavy, ungainly movements. When he reached the projection room he went into the separate steel-walled non-sync department. From the cupboard where spare valves were kept he took out one of a number of textbooks. They were his own property, the study of which at odd times had made him such a good technician. Ultimately he had hopes of becoming a chief projectionist in a really lush cinema.

'Sounds make patterns,' he muttered, his brows down. 'No doubt of that. And if that pattern I found in the dust was not made by sound I'll chuck myself off the fire escape!'

He turned the pages of the textbook and stopped when he came to the chapter on *Patterns Made By Sound*. There was a full page of geometrical designs, some of them looking rather like snowflakes. He read the context carefully:

The varied designs can all be produced by drawing a violin bow across the edge of a fixed plate on which some fine powder or sand has been sprinkled. The plate is of thin metal. Each plate is attached at its centre to a stand, and when the bow is drawn rapidly across the edge, parts of the sand vibrate into the designs shown. The higher the vibrations per second, the more intricate — and often the more lovely — becomes the resultant design. Even a bell ringing near the sand can produce designs, without recourse to a violin bow.[1]

Sid scratched the back of his thick neck and contemplated the designs again. None of them resembled the design he had seen. These, by comparison, were simple. The intricacy of the dust designs had been the main thing that had impressed him.

'But how?' he asked himself, putting the book back in the cupboard. 'The still-frame hasn't been in here for more than a fortnight, and in that time we haven't had any film which contained any particularly loud music, the only thing likely to produce a design like that. No musicals . . . or anything.'

His memory returned to the screws, which had moved from one end of the frame to the other and left a trail in the designed dust as they had travelled.

---

[1] *With acknowledgements to Charles Ray's 'Popular Science'.*

His perplexity deepened.

'Must have been vibration . . . somehow,' he mused. 'But there just isn't vibration up here — not that intense, anyway.'

He gave up thinking about it for the time being, but the matter returned to his mind during the matinee.

'Vibration,' he repeated to himself. 'Vibration which moved screws and drew complicated designs in the dust. Same sort of vibration might have brought down that globe that hit and killed Vera . . . '

At the moment be was absorbed by the pure mechanics. The thought of a *deliberately* produced vibration had not even occurred to him. But he certainly had not been satisfied with the opinion of the experts at the inquest, and he felt that quite by chance he had happened on a new line of enquiry. In fact he —

'I say,' Billy interrupted, lacing the machine that Terry usually ran. 'What's supposed to be the matter with this machine?'

'Matter?' Sid sounded vague. He found

190

it hard to bring his thoughts back to everyday things.

'Yes — matter! Terry's been messing about with this old cement mixer for two nights, hasn't he? What's he supposed to have done with it? Anyway, what was wrong with it in the first place — or is it a top secret?'

'I never really asked him,' Sid answered, shrugging. 'He said something about the take-up being wrong. Seems to be okay now so he must have fixed it.'

Billy muttered something, but Sid did not hear him. His thoughts had been deflected on to something else. A take-up repair would not demand *two nights' work*. Hardly more than ten minutes. Must have been something much more complicated wrong with the machine. Anyway, it seemed to be running all right now.

'Billy . . . ' Sid looked at the youth as he carboned up the arc. 'Have we had any particularly noisy films during the last fortnight? Advertisements or features? Brassy noisy interval or overture music?'

'Not as far as I know.' Billy did not

even hesitate. 'Most of the stuff we've been running has been all talk and no sense. Only decent thing I've seen in the last fortnight was that reel about the bathing beauties. There was one shot which — '

'Can you remember,' Sid interrupted, 'if the sound has been extra loud at any time?'

'I'm not up here much to be able to judge.'

'Mmm, I forgot that.'

'As far as I know,' Billy added, 'the sound has been stuck around fifty Jezebels.'

'Decibels you dimwit! Get yourself educated!'

'Okay, I'll consider it — Where's all this leading, anyhow? Who the heck cares what sort of films we're running so long as we're paid for 'em?'

'I care. I've something on my mind.'

'First time, I'll bet.' Then Billy hopped out and slammed the spring door before reprisals could be taken.

'The vibration couldn't come from one of the pictures we've had,' Sid said, recapitulating to himself. 'Yet, if it was a vibration it's possible that it might have happened at the same time as that globe dropping on Vera. Nothing like vibration to bring down a globe . . . What were we running at the time?'

His mind went back over the fatal evening and he frowned more than ever.

'That reminds me!' He pressed the button that rang the bell in the winding room below. Billy poked his head round the door in a moment or two.

'No you don't, apeman!' he said warily. 'You've only sent for me so you can beat the tar out of me! I'm not that crazy!'

'Stop clowning for a moment and come here,' Sid ordered. 'I want to ask you something.'

Billy shuffled in and kept his distance. Sid eyed him.

'Was that Fitz Travelogue we had at the back of last week a good copy?' Sid asked.

'Good? Sure it was! Technicolor usually is. Why?'

'I'm wondering why it broke on Saturday night.'

Billy rubbed the end of his nose.

'Hmm, so it did, now you come to mention it. Terry played heck with me for not checking the film properly. Queer ain't the word for it. There wasn't anything *to* check with no joints in it. It was a plain whiz through, as far as I was concerned.'

Billy left the box again as Sid made no answer. Mechanically, Sid opened the top spool-box and looked at the turning reel. It had only travelled half way yet: he had plenty of time to think before the changeover.

And the harder he thought the more complicated the problem seemed to become. Billy had been right, of course. A film without a joint in it could *not* break — and certainly not before it got to the top sprocket. Lower down — well, *perhaps*, but even then it was unlikely.

Yet Terry had said it *had* broken. He had made a grab at it and so avert trouble — so he had said — and he had mashed his first and second fingers in the process. It had been a fool thing to do. A projectionist of Terry's experience must have known that grabbing at a film when it had apparently broken could do no earthly good, not with the break so high up. Once snapped above the top sprocket the film had no chance of rethreading itself. A temporary shutdown was the only answer.

Yet Terry had said . . .

'Something queer,' Sid muttered, shaking his head.

And that broken piece of tumbler? Had it been the remains of a lemonade glass? If not, there remained one alternative — and after the matinee Sid looked for the alternative. He went into the washroom and looked for the tumbler that was usually on the shelf over the washbowl.

When he found it was missing his thoughts came to a full stop. They had to, mainly because he did not dare to believe the disquieting speculation that was trying to take shape in his mind.

* * *

When Sid arrived at the cinema next morning he found Terry looking extremely cheerful after his day off in the fresh air.

'There might be some news about

those new houselight fixtures this morning,' he said. 'Once they come we've a long job on our hands, Sid, changing the old fixtures. Be a good thing done, though. Funny how a life has to be lost before anything sensible is arrived at. I've given warning about those heavy fixtures dozens of times.'

'Seems to me,' Sid said slowly, 'that there's nothing particularly funny about a life being lost, no matter how you look at it.'

Terry glanced at him curiously. 'Still got Vera on your mind, eh? Well, I can't say I blame you. Incidentally, it's her funeral this morning isn't it? What are you going to do about it?'

'Nothing.'

'But — '

'I said nothing!' Sid snapped, his eyes brightening. 'I just couldn't bear seeing her put down.'

He was silent for a moment or two, then he played the first move in a game he had thought out for himself. He said:

'Kathy Gatty told me yesterday that we've got resonance in the hall speakers.'

In actual fact Kathy Gatty had never said anything of the sort, but since this was her day off she couldn't be asked for verification. Sid knew it. His main wish was to examine the loudspeakers behind the screen and see if there was any possible reason for a mysterious vibration. He could not investigate without a plausible reason and his chief's sanction, so —

'Resonance?' Terry repeated, frowning. 'Queer! There ought not to be, unless a chain's come loose.'

'I thought of having a look this morning,' Sid said.

'Okay. Go to it.'

Sid turned to go, then he hesitated. 'Oh, by the way. Do you know where the tumbler is out of the washroom? I had to make a paper cup yesterday when I wanted a drink.'

'Tumbler?' Terry stared for a moment, then he gave a start. 'Oh yes, the tumbler! I broke it a while back — on the bowl. I intended to replace it and then forgot. Sorry about that.'

'Okay. Just as long as we know . . . ' Sid

went on his way, satisfied on one point at least. Terry had been responsible for the missing tumbler, and had admitted it. But had it been broken on the bowl of the *washroom?* That piece of glass in the Circle . . .

Terry stood frowning for a moment or two after Sid had gone. The bit about the tumbler had caught him off guard, yet he felt that his reply had been adequate. His mind veered off into speculations for a moment, then returned to the everyday. He glanced at Billy, industriously checking a trailer film.

'Have good shows yesterday?' Terry inquired.

'Oh, sure! Couldn't be anything else with me rewinding, could there? Only thing was, I couldn't get much out of Sid.' Billy gave a sigh. 'He was about as cheerful as a duck waiting for a cloudburst.'

'That's normal with him, and he's been worse since Vera was killed.'

Billy tested a film joint and nodded to himself. Then he went on talking.

'I don't think it was Vera he was

bothering about,' he said. 'He hardly mentioned her. He seemed to be thinking a lot about Walt Disney's 'Fantasia'.'

Terry gazed blankly. 'Fantasia'? What on earth are you talking about?'

'Search me! You'd better ask Sid. I always thought he was a bit mental: now I'm sure of it.'

Billy finished his job and then went clattering up the steps to clean out the projection room. Terry stood where he was, his eyes hard as be pondered.

'Fantasia'? What conceivable reason could Sid have for remembering a film as old as that?

Finally, Terry threw the matter on one side. Did not signify anyway. Sid must have been talking 'shop'. Nothing more in it than that —

'You there, Terry?' It was the voice of Mark Turner at the base of the projection room steps.

'Yes, Mr. Turner.' Terry moved quickly. 'Coming.'

He hurried from the winding room and caught Mark Turner as he descended the main staircase. In silence they both went into the office. As a rule, Turner was calm and pleasant, with a friendly smile. Today there was a difference. He looked exceptionally annoyed.

'Terry, I've had a letter from the Zenith Distributors,' he said curtly, sitting down at his roll top desk. 'They've sent me a complaint that that Fitzpatrick Travelogue we ran in the latter half of last week is ruined. They say the sound track is one mass of scratches and it's impossible to run it at any cinema again . . . What's the explanation?'

Turner indicated the letter in question. It lay in the centre of the blotter. Terry remained calm though he looked worried. Things were working out just as he had anticipated they would.

'You mean ruined all through?' he asked, conveying the impression that he was trying to think of a reason for the mishap.

'From start to finish, so they say. It's going to cost me something like fifty pounds to have a new copy made — or rather the renters will get it made and charge it to me. That sort of thing doesn't improve one's profits, Terry. What have you to say about it?'

'There's only one thing I can think of,' Terry replied at length. 'As you know, I stayed behind for a couple of nights last week to try and fix up my machine — Number One. It's been running badly on the take-up. I thought I'd fixed it since the matinee ran okay on Saturday, and there seemed to be no trouble on the Saturday night — except for that break. But the sound was okay — '

'It was all right in the hall, certainly,' Turner agreed. 'I was listening to it. You remember I buzzed you when the Travelogue broke. How did that *happen*, by the way?'

'I've no idea. I imagine it was a mechanical defect.' Terry contemplated the plaster on his damaged fingers. 'I can only think the machine needs an overhaul, or something. Since the sound was all right in the hall when we ran the film, it can only mean that the track got scratched once it had got below the sound gate. That's perfectly obvious. And that seems to me like take-up trouble.'

'I see.' Turner wished he were more familiar with the technicalities. 'Well, you're the chief. What's the answer?'

'I'm afraid there isn't one,' Terry said deliberately. 'The renters are in the right, of course, and our trouble is mechanical.'

'What about Dixon, the service engineer? Why don't we get him to look at the machine? This trouble may happen again and then we'll be in a real mess — '

'I'm pretty sure it won't happen again, sir. Whatever the trouble was, it hasn't recurred. We've run perfect shows since Sunday night.'

Turner thought it out, stroking his underlip.

'Queer,' he muttered. 'Decidedly queer. There have been no complaints about the feature picture, which ran *after* the Travelogue. Seems that the trouble was just on that one Travelogue film. In fact, we seemed to pick up a whole load of trouble about that time. What with the film breaking, then the houselight coming down and killing Miss Holdsworth . . . '

'Yes, sir,' Terry agreed, his face rather

gaunt. He vaguely wondered if Mark Turner were piecing things together.

Evidently he was not. He was merely recanting. In any case, he had not the technical knowledge to fit things into place.

'All right, I'll have to pay,' he said finally. 'And for heavens' sake be more careful in future.'

'I will,' Terry assured him, and left the office. At the base of the stairs he hesitated, looking at Helen Prescott as she dusted the gilded radiator near the stalls entrance.

'Walking home with me at lunchtime?' she asked, smiling.

'Sure — be glad to. Seen Sid?'

'Sid? Why, yes.' Helen jerked her head. 'He went down the gangway to go backstage. About fifteen minutes ago. Haven't seen him since.'

'Thanks.'

Terry's mouth tightened at the corners. It ought not to take anything like fifteen minutes to discover if the speakers had a loose chain. Irritated, he strode down the gangway and finished his journey at the little door low down on the right hand side of the proscenium.

At the end of the backstage passage were the four steps leading to the stage behind the screen. Here, amidst swinging electric bulbs, surrounded by iron scaffolding, huge speakers, felting, and fuse-boxes, Sid was poking around with his torch. At every movement dust rose in fine clouds.

'What the hell are you doing all this time?' Terry demanded. 'Takes you long enough to locate the fault, doesn't it!'

'I haven't found it, and it's got me worried,' Sid replied, not in the least disturbed.

'You're not likely to find it, either,' Terry snapped. 'Kathy Gatty must have been imagining things. I can tell you right now that there's nothing wrong behind here. Come on upstairs, we've work to do.'

'Okay. You're the boss.'

Sid had no objections to leaving. He had satisfied himself that there was not the remotest sign here of anything that could have produced vibration. Since that was so, it meant that the vibration had somehow been produced when the show was running. He had not the vaguest idea *how*: the thought was simply there, awaiting development.

8

Visit to London

Moving clumsily, Sid followed Terry's tall figure out of the narrow passage and into the theatre. They walked up the gangway side by side.

'Say,' Terry said, glancing, 'Billy tells me that you spent all day yesterday remembering about Disney's 'Fantasia'. Is he crazy, or are you?'

Sid grinned. 'Maybe both of us are. I mentioned it, but I certainly didn't talk about it all day. Billy's simply trying to sound impressive. He remembered about 'Fantasia', whereas I couldn't.'

'Remembered about it?' Terry frowned. 'Why the hell should he want to do that? Anyway, he wasn't with us when we ran that film.'

Sid reflected. There was the tendency for the situation to get out of hand if he was not careful. What he did not tell, Billy certainly would. Have to forestall him —

'The whole thing came up,' Sid said, because I happened to remember a film which had a lot of designs in it.' He knew it was most unlikely that Terry had the slightest idea that there were designs in the dust on top of the Circle still-case. 'So I asked Billy if he could remember what film it might have been. Hence — 'Fantasia'.'

They had reached the stalls doorway before Terry asked another question.

'What should you want to remember about designs for?'

'Oh, just an idea.' Sid gave a shrug. 'I've a private ambition to become a cartoonist.'

Terry had not the chance to comment on this for at that moment Turner appeared in his office doorway. He signalled briefly.

'Sid — just a moment.'

'Coming, sir.' Sid went across the intervening space with his clumsy, loping walk. Terry stopped at the foot of the stairs and waited.

A thought clouded his mind. Surely

Turner was not going to tackle *Sid* about the damaged film? Sid, a technician, would start to think things. Terry had gambled on the quite logical possibility that, as chief, only *he* would be the one to be told that the film had been damaged. It was his responsibility entirely; nothing to do with the second projectionist — even less so since he had not run that particular machine.

Terry felt his brow becoming moist. He lighted a cigarette to steady his nerves.

Yet, in truth, nothing very startling was transpiring inside the manager's office. Turner turned to his desk as Sid followed him in. He picked up a slide in a cardboard carton.

'Take this toothpaste advert, Sid, and — Excuse me.'

Turner picked up the telephone as it rang noisily. Sid waited idly, not particularly interested in the conversation the manager was having with a local Councillor friend. His eyes travelled absently to the desk, and finally to a letter on the blotter. The letter was face up. Sid was not curious. He read the letter because there wasn't anything better to do at the moment.

Zenith Film Distributors.
Wardour Street, London.
August 26th 1957
M. Turner Esq.,
Cosy Cinema,
High Street, Bartonwick.
Dear Sir,
   We respectfully beg to draw your attention to the fact that the film Fitzpatrick Travelogue, on hire to you for the latter half of last week, is badly damaged. The sound track is so scratched from beginning to end of the film that it will be impossible for us to offer it on hire elsewhere. Since your logbook, signed by the chief projectionist, declares that the film was in perfect order when received, we must ask you to accept liability.
   Trusting to hear from you at your early convenience, and with regrets,
Yours faithfully,
   Per Pro Z.P.D./JK

Sid read the letter through again with growing incredulity — then he switched his attention back to Turner as he put the 'phone down, on its cradle.

'Now, where was I?' Turner asked. 'Oh, yes — about this slide. It's for toothpaste, and will replace the one you have now. Run this until the last day of December. No longer. You're in charge of the slides so it's your responsibility.'

'Right, sir,' Sid promised, and picking up the slide he left the office. The contents of that letter on the desk were still vivid in his mind. The sound track of the Fitzpatrick Travelogue scratched from end to end —

'What did he want?' Terry asked, at the foot of the stairs. 'He kept you long enough, didn't he?'

'Only this slide.' Sid held it up in the carton. 'He had to answer the 'phone to Johnson — that pot-bellied Councillor who always gets in without paying.'

'Oh!' Terry stubbed out his cigarette and put the remaining stub in his cigarette case. 'That all?'

'Sure. What else did you expect?'

210

Terry did not answer and Sid waited to see if Terry said anything about the Travelogue film. Or had he even been told yet? Sid had no idea. Certainly Terry did not make any remark about it — and yet, since Turner did not call him at all, it seemed that he *had* been told. Why should he want to keep the news of a damaged film all to himself? Usually he broadcast all complaints about films, if only to lessen the blow for himself.

'We'd better get upstairs,' Terry said, and Sid gave a nod.

So things went on until at last Sid could stand the suspense no longer. He asked a direct question whilst he and Terry were lounging on the 'bridge' enjoying a mid-morning cigarette.

'Seen the boss today, Terry?'

Terry knew he had to answer the question truthfully. Helen Prescott had seen him leaving the manager's office, so no evasion was possible.

'Sure I've seen him, to fix up next week's programme. Just after you'd gone backstage. Why?'

211

'I just wondered if you thought he looked worried.'

'Not more so than usual. Why?'

'Oh — nothing.'

The subject dropped. Sid was satisfied, but Terry was not.

He failed to see the reason for the question anyway. Sid, for his part, was quite sure that Terry could never have seen Turner and not have been told about the ruined film. So Terry *was* keeping the news to himself . . . but for why? As he stood and mused Sid felt passingly grateful for the fact that thoughts cannot be read. Then at length he looked at his watch.

'Hour to go,' he announced. 'I think I'll get some more work done on that still-frame. Unless you need me?'

'No, I don't need you. Go ahead.'

With a nod Sid went up the four iron steps and vanished in the projection room. There was the thud of the spring door as he departed. Terry remained where he was, disturbing thoughts drifting across his mind.

In the meantime, Sid got the ladder

from the orchestra pit and carried it up to the Circle. When he reached the top of the still-frame he considered the pattern in the dust . . . It was there unchanged, just as it had been the day before. And since then there had been two performances, so certainly nothing contained in *their* sound had been strong enough to produce vibration.

For a while Sid stood and looked at the designing, then with his hand he obliterated it and smeared the dust in all directions. If Terry ever came to look up here he would never know whence had come the urge to learn more about Walt Disney's 'Fantasia'.

Slowly, as he worked on the frame, Sid began his mental processes again . . . For instance, why had Terry snatched at that film? *Why?*

Sid stopped screwing and cast his mind back. His big face took on an expression of wonder, hardening into grim lines. What about Helen Prescott? Now he came to think of it he had remarked that Helen was seated down there, and not Vera. After that Terry had suddenly and

213

mysteriously panicked, even to the extent of lacerating his fingers in the projector. Terry liked Helen a good deal: everybody was aware of it. He had hated Vera Holdsworth. Everybody was aware of that, too.

'No!' Sid whispered, struggling again with the sinister thought at the back of his mind. 'No! It's too fantastic!'

His mind travelled further. For two nights Terry had stayed behind at the cinema, ostensibly to repair his machine. If he had repaired it, why had the film been ruined? And further, if the film had sounded perfect in the hall — as it had, or there would have been complaints from Turner — it could not possibly have been ruined afterwards except by deliberate intent!

Sid knew perfectly well that once a film gets below the sound gate it has only a pair of twin nylon rollers and a sprocket drum to traverse before winding itself on the take-up spool. No possible mechanical defect could make it run so that its sound track would become badly scratched — and there was even less chance of it with a projectionist who took such a pride in his job as Terry.

Billy had had no accidents when stripping the film off. He was not to blame. The defect had been *made*. It was *deliberate*. Why? Sid stood motionless on top of the ladder.

In that moment he was convinced of another fact. Vera had not died because the globe had accidentally dropped. She had died *because Terry had arranged it*!

Sid got down from the ladder, lighted one of his Turkish cigarettes, and then stood thinking harder than he had ever done in his life before. Though there was no longer any doubt in his mind but what Terry had created the tragedy, the motive for it seemed infinitely remote.

Sid knew Terry intimately. In a projection room, perhaps more than any other business, the closeness of association bares every facet of a man's character. Terry was a clever electrician, an ingenious thinker, but prone to sudden moments of wildness when his worse side became revealed. He had had a bad time of it with Vera, certainly, but had it been

215

bad enough for him to think of . . . murder?

'It hardly seems possible,' Sid muttered. He shook his head slowly. 'It just doesn't . . . unless . . . '

He became silent, looking at the Turkish cigarette smouldering between his fingers. It brought back memories of another Turkish cigarette, which had been in the manager's office after the burglary. Terry had not admitted that he had smoked it until he had been forced — and as far as Sid knew there was no guarantee that even then Terry had made any effort to clear him. It had been a strange act — and certainly not one of a friend.

£205 had been stolen. Terry had lost £200 at the races. The police were presumably still investigating and had not arrived at any decision . . .

Gradually, Sid worked his way back to the death of Vera. Normally, there was no motive strong enough to warrant murder by accident; but *were* the conditions normal? Vera had been with Terry at the races. There now loomed the definite possibility that Terry might — for all his denials — have been the thief. And if by some strange chance Vera had known of that fact . . .

'It's possible,' Sid breathed, 'that Vera might have said something at home. I'd better go and have a word with her folks at lunchtime — and find out how the funeral went on, too. I'm going to get to the bottom of this if it's the last thing I do!'

★   ★   ★

When Sid returned upstairs he tried not to give the slightest hint of the disturbing thoughts passing through his mind. He found Terry idling about the projection room, and Billy was in the non-sync department, polishing slides with a duster, to which he added a trace of spit as required.

'Still-frame finished?' Terry inquired.

Sid mused for a moment, then: 'Tell me something, Terry. Did you ever get this machine right? You stayed behind for a couple of nights to fix it. I've been meaning to ask you what you accomplished . . . ' and Sid nodded to the machine against which he was leaning.

'It's all right now,' Terry answered, his voice level.

Sid looked at the machine critically, opened the small, square door of the sound-gate, and contemplated the mechanism in the cavity beyond.

'It ran all right yesterday,' Sid remarked. 'But Billy was asking about it and it occurred to me that — '

'What the devil's it got to do with Billy?' Terry snapped.

Billy poked his untidy head round the adjoining steel wall of the non-sync room,

'Who's taking my name in vain?' he demanded. 'I work around here, remember. No harm in my asking about that old cement mixer, was there?'

'Of course there wasn't,' Sid answered him. 'Shows you've got an interest in your job, anyway . . . ' Sid's gaze strayed back to Terry — a steady, analytical stare. 'You don't have to jump on the kid like that, Terry. He only wanted to know if the machine was okay, same as I want to know now. We have to run it when you're not here, remember.'

Terry forced a grin even though the glint of suspicion remained in his eyes.

'Take-up trouble, that's all,' he said. 'I fixed it. I put a new chain wheel on the spindle. There'll be no more trouble.'

Sid nodded. 'Fair enough.'

He dropped the subject, but Terry continued to look at him.

Sid had asked perfectly normal questions, as one projectionist to another. There was no conceivable reason, Terry told himself, why Sid should read anything else into the matter.

'Blimey, it's three minutes to twelve!' Billy gasped suddenly. 'Time we shoved off for dinner. I'm as empty as a barrel.'

'Your head or your stomach?' Sid asked him — then he followed the youth downstairs to the winding-room for his jacket.

Terry joined them in a moment or two. He did not speak. He was busy with his own thoughts, and since Sid had also plenty on his mind he did not attempt conversation either. Sid left the building by way of the fire escape, with the talkative Billy for company.

Sid did not go straight home. Instead he detoured to the Holdsworth house in Malvern Road. Mrs. Holdsworth, a big, raw-boned woman with high cheekbones, opened the door.

'Oh, hello Sid!' She jerked her big, greying head. 'Come in.'

Sid followed her into the untidy living room. Mrs. Holdsworth was in the midst of laying lunch.

'Well, what's wrong?' she asked briefly. 'I don't think much of the time you've picked, either. I've work to do getting dinner ready.'

'Don't let me stop you,' Sid murmured, and he followed her into the back kitchen whilst she hovered over the gas stove. 'I have one or two questions to ask — about Vera.'

Mrs. Holdsworth's hard, severe face glanced towards him.

'About Vera, eh? Doesn't seem you've shown much interest in her memory since she was killed. You didn't even come to the funeral this morning.'

220

'Only because I didn't want to see her buried. I couldn't have stood it . . . I suppose everything went off according to plan?'

'Good as you could expect. Not many mourners. Our family hasn't got many friends. Vera hadn't many, either . . . Took about an hour, then I came back. My old man went straight on to work afterwards.'

'I see.' Sid found the matter-of-fact, even callous, way in which Mrs. Holdsworth referred to the funeral of her daughter decidedly disturbing.

'Well, Sid, what do you want, anyway?' This came after a long interval whilst Mrs. Holdsworth prodded the potatoes in a pan.

'I happen to be interested in one or two things,' Sid said. 'Can you remember if Vera went back to the cinema at all any night last week? After the show was over?'

Mrs. Holdsworth reflected and then went back into the living room. Sid followed her dutifully.

'Sit down.' She jabbed a finger towards a bentwood chair. 'Since you've got this far, I suppose it can't do any harm for you to know the rest.'

'Rest?' Sid repeated.

'Yes. Now Vera's dead it can't make any difference far as I can see.'

Sid sat down and stared at her, trying to fathom things out.

Mrs. Holdsworth gave one big, self-piteous sniff and then went on:

'I know what you're thinking, Sid — that Vera pinched that two hundred quid from the cinema.'

'I — er — ' Sid stopped, not really quite sure what he was thinking. The notion of Vera being the thief had never occurred to him.

'I think she did,' Mrs. Holdsworth, said slowly, staring through the window on to the unglamorous back yard. 'I know she's dead, and I know she was my daughter, but she was deceitful! Yes, deceitful! I'd be a fool if I didn't admit it. I found her out many a time, right from being a little girl. I had no time for her, and that's plain speaking. Different with her father: she could do no wrong in his eyes. She was like her old man was Vera; not to be trusted.'

Sid had heard hints about Vera's home life before and drawn his own conclusions — but he had never heard things stated so baldly as this. He sat waiting, pondering, his eyes on Mrs. Holdsworth's harsh features.

'A week ago tonight — last Wednesday — she went back to the cinema after the night show,' Mrs. Holdsworth continued. 'Said she'd forgotten her cigarettes and wanted them urgent. We thought nothing of it. I don't smoke and neither does the old man — but he drinks like the devil to make up for it. Anyway, nothing would satisfy Vera but that she go and get them. It was after midnight when she got back. We asked her why she'd been so long and she said it was none of our business.'

'Then?' Sid asked, thinking.

'Next thing that happened we read in the paper about the burglary at the Cosy. Two hundred of the best stolen. I tackled Vera about it and she begged me and her father not to say that she had been back to the cinema for cigarettes. Naturally, we thought things but we promised to keep quiet. You don't give away your own flesh and blood in a crisis . . . '

Mrs. Holdsworth took her gaze from the yard and rested her elbow on the table edge.

'Yesterday,' she finished, setting her mouth, we got a letter from the Apex Furriers in Balton Street. It seems they'd seen in the paper about the accident which killed Vera and they wanted to know what was to be done about a fur coat she'd ordered for the winter, and for which she'd paid one hundred and fifty pounds. Amongst the things in her handbag were fifty pounds in notes, too. There was only one answer to that, Sid. She stole the money from the cinema.'

Sid stroked his eyebrow and said nothing.

'I'm telling you, Sid, because it can't make any difference now. But it's as plain as can be. She had a passkey to the cinema. She must have had it all weighed up.'

'Circumstantially it does look like it,' Sid admitted.

'Eh?' The hard grey eyes studied him. '*Circumstantially*? Facts are facts, aren't they?'

'Oh, sure they are — but if Vera meant to rob the cinema I can't see why she told you she was going back there. It doesn't seem logical, somehow.'

'Don't see what else she could have done. If she hadn't have come home first we'd have been enquiring after her — so she thought up the only excuse she could. She knew we'd stand by her when the police enquired. And we'd never have really known at all except for her getting killed and the business of the fur coat coming to light. You must have guessed the truth, too, otherwise you wouldn't have come asking if she ever went back to the cinema. It can't do any good if you spread the news, Sid. And if you're the sort of chap I think you are, you won't.'

'No, I won't,' Sid promised. He rubbed the back of his neck and then made a rueful admission. 'This has come as one mighty big shock to me, Mrs. Holdsworth — no doubt about it. Anyway, thanks for telling me . . . Now I've got to be going. Time's getting short.'

★　★　★

Sid returned half an hour too early for the evening show, a particular purpose in his mind. He went immediately to No. 1 Machine and, squatting down beside the gear chainwheel — rather like the gearwheel of a bicycle — he studied the wheel's serial number.

'MCD/456982,' he murmured, writing it down. 'Now, let's see what we get.'

He hurried down to the winding room and from a top shelf took the book in which were entered all alterations or new additions to the projection side of the plant. In no other way was it possible to keep a check on equipment, and each entry was counter-signed by Mark Turner.

Sid's eyes narrowed as he examined the items under Machine No. 1. Not a single addition had been made to the machine for three years, and the take-up chainwheel had been fitted at that time by Clifford Dixon, the service engineer. The wheel's number was listed as MCD/456982.

'The dirty liar!' Sid slammed the book savagely and threw it back on the shelf — then he got a hold of his temper quickly. He left the cinema again for he had no wish to be caught here ahead of time. Less than ever did he wish to give grounds for appearing suspicious about anything. Without doubt, Terry had taken too much for granted in saying he had fitted a new chainwheel, or else he had for the moment forgotten that all such new fixtures had to be entered up and counter-signed.

For twenty minutes Sid prowled about in the sunlight of the hot August evening; and then he returned to the cinema at the usual time. He found Terry in about the same mood as earlier, neither unpleasant nor cordial. Plainly he was preoccupied with many things.

Sid went on with his job as usual, talking but little, spending most of his time in deep thought. He still had no idea why it should have been necessary to kill Vera if she had taken the £205. Once the astounding thought occurred to him that maybe Terry had committed the murder to save him — Sid — from marrying a thief. As soon as the idea occurred Sid flatly rejected it. There must have been a very real reason for wanting Vera out of the way. What? The only likely one seemed to be that Terry had stolen the money and . . . Perhaps Vera had seen him do it, or had known of it.

Sid's eyes began to brighten a little. Yes, it *was* possible! Her own £200 might have another explanation, which, now she was dead, would never be explained. That being so, it could be that she had returned to the cinema, just as she had said, to get her cigarette case — and surprised Terry in the midst of his theft. It was, to Sid, still a highly illogical factor that Vera, intending to rob the cinema, would ever have told her parents that she was *going* there.

Towards the end of the reel on his machine an idea struck Sid. When he had summoned Terry for the changeover to No. 1 machine he took the film out of his own projector and carried it down to the winding room. Billy, it being the mid-week film stripping night, was busy spinning off films into their transit cases.

'I'll do this one,' Sid said briefly, dumping the reel on the bench. 'Give you a change. Go and thread my machine up, will you?'

'Okay, apeman. Thanks for the break.' And Billy scuttled off up the stone steps.

Sid waited until he heard the spring door of the projection room slam, then he glanced towards the three jackets hanging on the wall pegs. His own jacket, Billy's — and Terry's. In one stride he reached Terry's jacket and felt through the pockets. Normally, it was an act that he would have scorned to do — but things were normal no longer. He had got to *know*, by any means, foul or fair.

The first thing he encountered was Terry's wallet in the inside pocket. He tugged it out and examined it quickly, still keeping his ear cocked for the return of Billy down the steps.

There was a union card, some silver, receipts for sub-standard movie projectors, a calendar, a race card — Sid read the calendar's front earnestly. It conveyed the information on which he had hoped he might alight. On the calendar front it said:

*This will be a Lucky Year for You if You
Place Your Bets with George Naylor.
Denham Street,
Bartonwick
Tel:612*

'So that's his bookie,' Sid breathed,
putting the calendar back in the wallet,
and the wallet in the jacket. 'I never knew,
and I daren't ask him. I don't even know
if he ever paid that two hundred he owed.
All Vera told me was that he'd phoned to
a bookie but she didn't know the bookie's
name. George Naylor, eh? Just possible,
too, that Naylor had outstanding debts
against Terry amounting to two hundred,
which made theft the only way out . . . '

Sid clenched his big fist. 'I've got to
find out by some means if Terry really
had justification for stealing two-hundred
— and if he had, it means that Vera *could*
have caught him at it. Then, rather than
have her speak he polished her off!'

Sid turned back to the job of stripping
off the reel he had brought down. He was
resolved that he would see George Naylor
at lunchtime next day — and since

George Naylor had never seen Sid before he gave him the bland, welcoming smile he usually reserved for potential clients.

Sid eyed him as he stood at the other side of the desk. His sandy hair was on end, as usual, and there was dogged resolution on his face.

'Well, young man?' Naylor sat back in his swivel chair. 'Something I can do for you?'

'As a matter of fact, there is. First, get one thing straight: I'm not here to place a bet.'

'Well, that's too bad. What *do* you want? I'm a busy man.'

'Do you know a chap named Terry Lomond?' Sid asked.

'Uh-huh.' Naylor lighted a cigarette and waited.

'He owes you two hundred quid, doesn't he?'

'Not any more he doesn't. And what the hell's it got to do with you?'

'I'm a friend of his.'

'A friend, eh? Well, where's all this leading? I got paid, and I'm satisfied. Anything more to it?'

'Might be.' Sid was not easy to shake from his purpose. 'I'm trying to figure out where he got his two hundred from . . . I work with him at the Cosy Cinema.'

Naylor drew at his cigarette. 'Look here, young man, it isn't my custom to give away clients' business to strangers. You sort of surprised me into saying Lomond had paid up all that was owing.'

'*All* that was owing?'

'That's what I said. It sounds as though he can't have told you much even if you are his friend.' Naylor flicked ash on the floor. 'He lost his money. Somebody pinched it. Evidently he didn't tell you that?'

Sid stood thinking. 'No . . . No, he didn't.'

'All right then, he must have borrowed it from somebody.'

'Yes, I suppose he must,' Sid agreed. 'All right, thanks for the information. And next time you see Terry you don't have to tell him I've been here. We have to work together and he'd probably raise the roof.'

'I shan't tell him anything,' Naylor said.

Sid went, absorbed by a new line of

thought. The suspicion he had formed that Terry had had a reason for needing £200 had been confirmed. Very best reason in the world! To pay off his bookie. And his wallet, in which the money had presumably been, had been stolen. Yet now it was back in his jacket!

Sid stopped at the end of the cul-de-sac and rubbed his heavy jaw slowly.

'Yes, but even now . . . ' he mused. 'What would have happened if Terry had not paid up? The bookie couldn't have done very much. Unlikely that Terry would have lost his job — Why such desperation to get that two hundred at any price, I wonder? Why risk burglary and imprisonment for it when, had the worst happened, he could have pleaded the Gaming Act and escaped?'

Sid's thoughts slowed down and came to a halt. He had just realized that he was looking straight at Terry himself, with Helen Prescott by his side.

9

Further investigations

'Well!' Helen exclaimed in surprise. 'Just look who's here! If it isn't our tough second projectionist in person!'

Terry said nothing for a moment. He glanced down the cul-de-sac and then back at Sid's face. Sid could not help his vague look of consternation. He was never very good at controlling his emotions.

'Making a bet?' Terry asked quietly.

'Bet?' Sid lost his vagueness. 'No. Why should I?'

'Deduction,' Terry explained dryly. 'You're not interested in antiques or needlework, and the only other person doing business in this street is a bookie — and you're coming *up* the street.'

'I never knew you gambled, Sid,' Helen remarked, in mock reproof. 'Mr. Turner will burn up if he ever finds out.'

'Look here, what *is* this?' Sid demanded,

seeking his usual juggernaut way out of a tight corner. 'If it comes to that I might as well ask you two what *you* are doing here. It's a public street — '

'I'm going to make a bet.' Terry's voice was cold and level. 'I've a particular nag I fancy for today's two-thirty. My bookie is down the street here — or do you know that already?'

'Why should I?' Sid snapped. Then his gaze switched to Helen as she was beginning to look bewildered. 'You making a bet too, Helen?'

'Well, I'm risking thirty shillings — providing you don't mind! Or do you think a woman's place is in the cinema? Terry and I simply made up our minds to have a bet, so we came along to place it before going to lunch.'

'Oh! Sorry, Helen. I didn't mean to sound brusque.'

'What's the idea, Sid?' Terry asked, his voice edged with steel.

'Idea? I don't — '

'Oh, yes you do! You don't bet; you're not the type. You're spying on me and my affairs, that's what! Do you take me for a damned fool? You're not in this street by accident. Ten to one you've been to see George Naylor, and I demand to know why!'

'Terry!' Helen gripped his arm. 'Hold on a bit!'

'I've no reason for pulling my punches!' Terry retorted. 'I've been suspicious of you for some time, Sid. The things you have been saying; the way you have been acting, the looking at me. What's it all about? What am I supposed to have done? Now's as good a time as any to have it out!'

'If you don't mind I prefer my lunch,' Sid answered, then with a nod to Helen he strode on his way.

Terry wheeled and watched him go, his lips a tight line.

'Terry, for heavens' sake!' Helen pulled at him urgently. 'What on earth did you have to blow up like that for? Why should Sid want to spy on you?'

Terry was silent for a while, inwardly regretting many of the things he had said.

'He just gets me down,' he muttered. 'Big, beefy dimwit! He's had it in for me ever since Vera was killed. Lord knows why! I even think he's got it in the back of his mind that I was responsible for it somehow.'

'But that's absurd! And certainly it isn't anything to get hot and bothered about. If he wants to think such horrible things — Well, let him!'

'Yes . . . ' Terry grinned slowly. 'Yes — let him! But I'll bet anything in the world that he's been finding things out about me from George Naylor — about me betting, I mean. What puzzles me is how Sid knew Naylor is my bookie. I've never mentioned it.'

Since Helen had run out of comments she contented herself with a jerk of her shoulder. Terry took hold of her arm and they began walking down the cul-de-sac in the direction of George Naylor's office. The look of puzzlement deepened on Helen's features.

'Terry, why should Sid want to find out about your betting? Especially when he doesn't have a flutter himself. Anyway, your bookie wouldn't give anything away, would he?'

237

'He might. I wouldn't trust Naylor across the street. I only deal with him at all because he's handy.'

Helen sighed and shook her head. 'It's all so confusing. None of it seems to make sense.'

Together, she and Terry entered Naylor's office. He glanced up at them from behind his desk and then gave a nod.

''Morning, Terry — Miss,' he added, looking at Helen.

'Here's seven pounds ten shillings,' Terry said, putting the money on the desk. 'To win on 'Echo' in the two-thirty.'

Naylor took the money and made out a receipt. He was looking puzzled.

'What's the idea? You usually 'phone in your bets. Your credit's okay with me, you know — up to a reasonable point, that is.'

'After the last mess I got into I prefer paying cash on the nail.'

Naylor shrugged. 'All right with me. Maybe it is safer than having it pinched — though who'd want to pinch seven pounds only I can't imagine.'

Helen frowned and Terry gave Naylor a grim look of warning.

The bookmaker remained complacent and perspiring.

'I just passed a pal of mine on the street,' Terry went on. 'Sid Elbridge. I have the idea he's been here. Am I right?'

'Big, hefty chap with sandy hair?'

'That's the man.'

'Yes — he came here.'

'Why?' Terry snapped. 'That's what I want to know. Did he try and find out things about me?'

Naylor smiled amiably. 'About you? Of course not! He came to put ten bob on the three o'clock — and I wouldn't even tell you that much, only you seem to be a friend of his.'

Terry hovered on a remark, but didn't say it. Instead he took Helen's arm.

'Right,' he said, looking at Naylor. 'See you later — to collect.'

Out in the street Helen darted a quick glance at Terry's grim face.

'Terry, it's no use you looking so savage! You know the truth now. You simply got all steamed up over nothing — and I still can't see why you had to get so excited anyway.'

239

'You can't eh?' Terry's voice was edgy. 'I'll stake everything I've got that that fat old swine was lying. He knows I'd never deal with him again if I thought he'd been talking behind my back.'

Helen laughed shortly. 'If you only put six pounds of your money and one pound ten of mine down every time, I shouldn't think he'd notice your departure.'

'Last time I bet it was two hundred pounds! Don't start making me out to be a miser. I bet big — when I can, that is.'

Helen said quietly: 'You've got quite a temper all your own, haven't you? And not the slightest reason for it, either. Sid places a bet, you jump to conclusions — though I don't see why — and now there's no bearing you!'

Terry did not answer. Walking slowly, they presently reached the end of the cul-de-sac.

'Tell me something, Terry — What did Naylor mean by saying it was better to pay up than have your money pinched?' Helen's face was thoughtfully serious. 'Why should it be pinched?'

'For heavens' sake, Helen, don't you

ever stop asking questions?'

'Not as long as I'm puzzled.'

'There's nothing to be puzzled about!' Terry spoke deliberately, as though to a none-too-bright child. 'Please realize that! If you're going to make mountains out of molehills I'm sorry I ever took you to that confounded office. I merely thought you might like to see a bookie in his native habitat.'

'It wasn't very edifying, was it?' Helen smiled rather cynically. 'I've got to cut down the street opposite,' she added, 'otherwise I'm going to be late for lunch. See you later.'

She was gone before Terry had the chance to speak again. He watched her slender figure darting across the road amidst the traffic. There was no short cut to her home just here, as far as could remember. It began to look as though she had walked out on him.

* * *

Sid was thoughtful as he ate his lunch. He had the fixed, concentrated look of a man

241

trying to puzzle out a profound riddle.

His mother, who knew his every mood, did not disturb him by asking questions. She assumed it was some technical problem and therefore no concern of hers.

Sid left ten minutes earlier than usual for the cinema, chiefly because he liked to do his thinking in the open air as he walked about. The major point still absorbing him was why Terry had committed burglary when at the worst he could have found a way to wriggle out of the difficulty. There also was the lesser, but still important point of the wallet. If it had been stolen, with money in it, how on earth had Terry ever got it back? And it was Terry's wallet. Sid knew it well.

When Sid reached the cinema that afternoon he found Terry already there, and in a grim mood. Sid met the cold stare of his eyes as he came into the winding room.

'Cheerful, aren't you?' Sid remarked shortly, hanging up his jacket.

'I came back early for one reason,' Terry retorted. 'So we can have things out before Billy gets here. It's no business of his.'

Sid thrust his hands in his trouser pockets and lounged across to where Terry was standing with his back to the winding bench.

'All right,' Sid gave a critical look. 'So you want to have things out. Where do you start?'

'Did you make a bet with George Naylor today, or didn't you?'

'What's it got to do with you?'

'Answer the question, can't you?'

Sid's expression changed. Dark anger came into his craggy face. 'Am I supposed to be on trial or something? Mind your own damned business!'

'I wish you'd do the same!' Terry blazed. 'I believe you went to see Naylor for only one reason — to try and get information from him about me! You think — and always have thought — that I pinched that two hundred and five quid from the boss's office. You've thought so ever since I kept quiet about that Turkish cigarette of yours, just because at that time I hardly knew what to say.'

'Supposing I did think that?' Sid asked. 'What do you think I could do about it? The police are handling the business, aren't they? How much more could I do?'

'You might have an angle.'

'If you didn't commit the burglary why are you worrying?' Sid gave one of his direct looks. Then he added, 'Look here, if you've done nothing wrong at any time what makes you jump to the conclusion that I'm spying on you, and trying to find things out, as you call it. You wouldn't give a hoot if your conscience were clear.'

'Are you insinuating that it isn't?' Terry snapped.

'I'm no psycho-analyst,' Sid shrugged. 'Think it out for yourself.'

Terry breathed hard, then he made a tremendous effort. 'I — I suppose I'm acting like an idiot,' he muttered. 'Can't entirely help it, though.'

There were sounds of clumsy feet on the iron fire escape outside to the accompaniment of the latest rock 'n roll tune, atrociously rendered. In a moment or two Billy came blundering into the winding room by the emergency doorway, a broad grin on his hastily washed face.

'Hiya, killers,' he greeted. 'Smashing day to take a girl out to the swimming pool. Maybe I will tomorrow.'

Terry and Sid both stood gazing at him, trying to reconcile the utter inconsequence of his thoughts. When neither of them spoke Billy drew his head into his jacket collar. As there was still no comment he looked at himself curiously.

'Smatter?' he asked. 'My slip showing?'

Terry roused himself. 'Go and get laced up,' he ordered. 'In case you don't know it you're five minutes late.'

'Couldn't help it. Irish stew weighs heavy in this weather. Took me all my time to paddle my 'bike — I'll catch up.'

Whistling shrilly, Billy pulled two reels out of the bin, shouldered them, and then went clattering up the steps to the projection room. Without a word to Terry, Sid followed suit. Billy turned a puzzled face as Sid came in.

'Say, apeman, what's the matter with Terry?'

'No idea,' Sid answered, and set about the task of threading his own machine.

'If you ask me, he's had the brush off,' Billy decided. 'Some girl — perhaps Hel Prescott — doesn't think much of his sunburned dial when she gets close to it. I know I don't.'

'Will you stop nattering?' Sid pleaded wearily.

'Okay,' Billy agreed, beaming. 'I was only trying to make the joint a little less like the morgue . . . Oh, you tak' the high road and I'll tak' the low road, and I'll be in the Cosy before you — '

'For heavens' sake stop that unholy row!'

Billy did not. He went on singing lustily in a curious vascillating tenor-baritone.

'For trouble it is there, and there'll be many films on fire, in the bonny, bonny box of Terry Lomond . . . '

Sid pressed finger and thumb to his eyes and sighed. He quelled a desire to throw Billy out neck and crop. After all, that would hardly be fair. He knew nothing of what was going on — or of what *had* been going on. He was simply a happy teenager and therefore a natural-born nuisance. He went on singing lustily until Terry arrived and gave him a sour look.

Instant silence.

Sid did not speak for the rest of the afternoon — unless it was to make some reference to the running of the show. Most of the time he was making up his mind what he was going to do. Tomorrow, Friday, would be Billy's day off. That would mean, for Sid, that there would be ample opportunity to explore the winding room whilst there on the pretext of rewinding film as it came from the machines. Terry, forced to remain in the projection room, would run the show and would be unable to interfere.

★   ★   ★

After the matinee, Helen Prescott purposely delayed herself in the staff room. Stealthy trips to the half-way on the Circle staircase, a few yards from the staff room door, assured her that Terry was hanging about in the foyer, no doubt waiting for her — Until at last he grew tired of his vigil and departed, presumably to the café across the road. Helen went swiftly down the stairs and was

247

heading towards the stalls entrance doors — intent on escaping by an emergency exit — when Turner came out of his office. His soft hat was tilted at an angle and he was in the act of drawing on washleather gloves.

'Why, Helen! Are you only just going?'

Helen stopped, hesitated, and then turned. Her pretty face had a rather uneasy smile.

'Yes, Mr. Turner. I — er — I was delayed. A little trouble with my uniform.'

'You're sure you don't mean Terry Lomond?'

Turner came towards the girl, smiling. Helen found herself thinking what a placid face he had, how tastefully he dressed without overdoing it. No sudden flarings in his manner, either — no sharp glances of suspicion. He, for his part, was merely observing details that he had seen many times already — the dark blue eyes, delicately pink cheeks, and wealth of glossy black hair. Out of uniform and in her fancy summer frock, Helen cut a highly delectable figure.

'Terry?' Helen repeated, and then

dropped her eyes before Turner's steady gaze.

'Yes — Terry. You've been out with him quite a lot recently, haven't you? I've been noticing, and I'm wondering what happened to stop you going out with him today.'

'Oh, we . . . just disagreed about something.'

'And now what? Are you escaping to a café for tea?'

'No; I'm going home this time. Mother's expecting me.'

'Mmm, I see.' Turner reflected. 'Well, I'm sure there's no need for you to leave the building like a fugitive — and that is obviously what you intend to do. I'll walk with you as far as the corner of the road — unless you'll change your mind and have tea with me? I'm going to the Silver Grill . . . I've asked you lots of times, Helen; you know that.'

'I know, Mr. Turner, but — '

'I've taken the liberty of calling you Helen outside business hours,' Turner said. 'I think we'd escape a lot of formality if you called me Mark. In fact

I'd really appreciate it if you would.'

Helen laughed slightly. 'It sounds dreadfully out of place, somehow'

'Not really. Suppose I explain it to you? Shall we go? We may be late back otherwise.'

Turner switched off the lights, took Helen's arm, and they went out together through the main front doors. Helen glanced across the road and wondered if, from the rear of the café, Terry were watching the proceedings.

'You see, Helen,' Turner explained, in his unhurried voice, 'the cinema imposes certain restrictions upon me. I have to assume an air of authority, otherwise there would be chaos. I even have to be terribly formal towards you, so the others won't think there is any favouritism, which would automatically make your life unbearable . . . But none of that stops me falling in love with you.'

'Falling — in love with me?' Helen repeated.

'Certainly! I fell in love with you the day you came to ask for the job of usherette. Why shouldn't I? I'm still quite a young man, and even cinema managers

250

are capable of human emotions. As to the rest of the details — I'm just over thirty, and you're twenty-six. I know you are,' Turner added, 'because your union card says so!'

Helen half laughed, then she gave a rather bewildered glance.

'Oh, I know what you're thinking,' Turner went on. 'I am the owner, manager, and employer — and you're the employee. Well, what of it? I could cite many instances where the manager married his secretary, so the cinema owner marrying the usherette mightn't be unique. I'm in love with you — completely. What more do we want?'

'Our positions are — different,' Helen said, not at all sure if that was the right remark to make.

'I'm lucky, that's all — and you're not *quite* so lucky,' Turner replied. 'My father, a brewer in a big way of business, left me a large sum when he died. I was interested in films, so in spite of television competition I bought the Cosy. Commercially, I have been successful in this little town because I own the only picture house and there's but little, if any, competition from the big houses a few miles away. In spite of all this I'm not particularly happy, though. I have nobody with whom to share my good fortune. My mother died some years ago, and all I've got is a housekeeper. Stated simply, Helen, I'm looking for a wife — and I hope I've found her.'

They walked on for a while in silence.

'As a matter of fact, I don't quite know what to say,' Helen confessed. 'You've always been terribly nice to me, but I never realized — I sort of thought, when you came out of your shell, that you did it to stop me going about with Terry Lomond.'

'You're too nice a girl for Terry Lomond,' Turner said.

They came to a stop. They had reached the end of the road in which Helen's home stood.

''Bye for now, Helen,' Turner said. 'I'm only too sorry you can't come and have tea with me. Whenever you do decide to do so I'm ready.'

He shook hands, and then went on his way.

Helen looked after him thoughtfully, and then finished the short journey to her home. That evening, when she returned to the cinema, she found Terry waiting for her in the foyer. He eyed, her as she came towards him from the big front doors.

'The horse lost,' he said briefly. 'Thought you'd like to know — unless you've forgotten we ever backed the infernal nag?'

'As a matter of fact, I had,' Helen confessed. 'Well, that's that, isn't it?'

'As far as the horse is concerned, yes — but what I want to know is: what about us?'

Helen remained silent. Terry's eyes still fixed her. Then he said deliberately,

'I saw you leave this teatime with Turner, you know.'

'No law against it,' Helen replied, colouring a little.

'True, but at least let's come to an understanding. I know I behaved pretty unreasonably at dinnertime, and I notice you've avoided me since. I can only say that I'm sorry.'

Helen shook her head slowly. 'It's no

use, Terry. I don't think we fit into each other's ways, somehow. Let's leave it at that and try and remain just good friends.'

'So our over-dressed boss got away with it in the finish, did he?' Terry asked sourly. 'And some damned fools say that money isn't everything!'

'It isn't a case of money — '

'Oh, shut up!' Terry stalked away across the foyer. Helen watched him go, then she turned as the front doors opened to admit the impeccable Mark Turner himself.

* * *

The following day, once the matinee began, Sid put his pre-arranged plan into action. Upon each occasion that he had to come down to the winding room with the film he made a search of the cupboards under the bench wherein were stacked all the spare parts liable to be needed for breakdowns in the projection equipment.

He took careful note of what there was, wrote down each item in his pocket book, and then returned upstairs to do his turn

254

at a machine. In this manner, throughout the afternoon, he gathered a complete list of everything. In the evening, he went on to the next phase — checking the items besides those listed in the 'Spare Equipment' log book, all of which items had been initialled by Turner upon their arrival.

Time and again Sid came across blanks in his checking. By the time the last reel of the evening was on the machine he knew just how far short the spare equipment list was. Alone at his machine, Terry working down below, he studied the items which were missing and put the approximate price against each one.

'Three pairs of girder skates,' he muttered. 'Six sets of idler bearings, half a dozen amplifier valves, three sets of lenses and condensers . . . '

One after another the items followed. Sid's face was grim by the time he had finished adding up the list and approximate value.

'Four hundred quid's worth of stuff at least!' he told himself. 'This explains much! No wonder he didn't want any inquiry into his activities.'

He put his notebook back in his pocket — and only just in time for Terry came into the box again and, without a word, lounged through it and to the fire escape.

'I don't expect to be lucky enough to fit every confounded piece into place,' Sid muttered to himself. 'But I *am* sure that he took care of Vera by bringing a house-light down on her head. Somehow that vibration occurred during Fitzpatrick's Travelogue. I wonder what there was about that film that could do that?'

He thought back over it in every particular but could recall no startling reason why it had produced the effect it had . . . One thing was clear. There was nothing to be gained by guessing. The only possible way in which he could even hope to get anywhere near the answer was by examining the Fitzpatrick film for himself.

How? Without letting Terry know? And the film now back with the London renters? By this time it might have been destroyed, considering the atrocious condition it had been in.

'Only one thing for it,' Sid decided to himself. 'It'll be my day off on Monday. I'm going to pay a flying visit to Wardour Street in London and see what I can do.'

He straightened up on the final fade out of the feature picture and called to Terry. Terry came in and brought the houselights into being as the National Anthem played. A thud, and the snap of the arc shutter. The show was over for the night and the air of the box was blue with carbon fumes with their curious sickly sweet odour.

'Another day shot to pieces,' Sid commented, and pulled the lever which dropped the safety shutters over the portholes. 'The nights are drawing in, too,' he added, glancing through the still open fire escape doorway to where the darkness had settled thickly.

'You getting poetic, or what?' Terry asked him cynically, emerging from the non-sync room where the play-out record was transmitting 'Colonel Bogey.'

Sid folded his arms and leaned against the switch boxes.

'I'm trying to make things a bit more

257

amiable around here,' he explained. 'You may get some fun out of walking in and out of here like an undertaker, but *I* don't.'

Terry reflected moodily. Sid watched him. He was quite prepared to be pleasant, even though he knew what he did. It would be superficial geniality, though, disguising the quest on which he was engaged.

'I'm a bit off colour,' Terry lied finally, switching off the amplifiers as the record came to an end. 'Not bodily — just mentally. Helen's given me the air completely. It happened yesterday tea time.'

'There's no reason why you should take it out of me, is there?' Sid demanded. 'Or have you still got the crazy idea that I'm spying on you, or something?'

'I was wrong there,' Terry sighed. 'Sorry . . .'

Sid looked at his watch. 'I think we'd both better be getting home. Maybe a night's sleep will help the pair of us to think a bit differently.'

'Maybe you're right at that.'

As far as Sid was concerned, sleep only deepened his resolve to go the limit in discovering everything he could about Terry's strange actions prior to the death of Vera — but he took good care, the following day, to behave as though he had not a care in the world.

Saturday and Sunday would, in fact, have been tedious had not the new houselight fixtures arrived. By working mornings and staying after the night performance, Terry and Sid took down the old, clumsy fixtures and installed the new ones — each with a 300-watt lamp and a big vellum shade. Just after midnight on the Sunday the job was done.

Sid was up early on the Monday morning and took the 7-52 train to London, arriving in the capital at ten to nine. At ten o'clock he was in the manager's office at the Zenith Film Distributors.

The manager, a short, keen-featured man with rimless eyeglasses and a bald head, surveyed the big, quietly dressed young man who was shown into the office. Then he got up with outstretched hand.

'Good, morning, Mr. — er — I didn't quite get what name my clerk said.'

'Elbridge — Sidney Elbridge. I'm the second projectionist at the Cosy Cinema in Bartonwick'

'Cosy Cinema? Oh? Well, sit down, won't you?'

Sid nodded and accepted the cigarette offered him. The manager sat back in his chair.

'Cosy Cinema,' he repeated, musing. 'I seem to have heard of that somewhere.'

'Very probably,' Sid agreed. 'We ruined a Fitzpatrick film and you, with justification, made a row about it. That's why I'm here, as a matter of fact.'

'Of course!' The manager's eyes lighted. 'A ruined sound track, wasn't it? Yes, I remember.' He turned to the desk-phone and pressed a switch. 'Miss Carlton, bring me the file for the Cosy Cinema, Bartonwick, will you please?'

'Right away, Mr. Bennet.'

'Why,' Bennet asked, switching off, 'have you come here in person about it, Mr. Elbridge?'

'Well, as a matter of fact — '

Sid paused, not because he had no answer ready but the secretary had come in with the file. The manager glanced through the correspondence after the girl had gone out again.

'I really don't see . . . ' he said finally, puzzled. 'Mr. Turner, your manager, has accepted full liability for the film and has agreed to pay our account of fifty-two pounds, the cost of a new copy. What more is there to say?'

'I want to borrow the Travelogue film, if I may, and find out why it was ruined,' Sid explained calmly.

'But you know what the damage was. It was the sound track.'

'Yes, but I can't see how it could possibly have happened on the machines we've got. Nor has the trouble happened before — or since. Don't you see that if there is some defect in the machine we've got to find it, otherwise — without warning — the fault may come up again and we might really ruin a valuable copy of some kind, not knowing a thing about it until the film has been run. Rewind boys are not over careful in examining the condition of a sound track. In, fact they don't even look at it unless they're told to.'

'I see what you mean,' the manager nodded. 'You think there may be a fault in the machine which can only be detected by running through the film which was spoiled?'

'That's it,' Sid agreed, thankful that the manager had taken the burden on his own shoulders. 'Renters, cinema managers, and projectionists like to co-operate with each other if thereby they can raise the standard of efficiency. I'm asking you to help us out, if you will. All I need is the film, and I'll see it's returned the moment I've tested it.'

Bennet considered for a moment or two. 'You say you're the second operator. Why doesn't your chief come instead of you?'

Sid smiled. 'As a matter of fact neither he nor the manager know I've made this trip — and I'm hoping you won't tell them, either. I think my own bad repair work may be at the back of the trouble, and that's why I want to rectify the damage before a worse thing happens.'

'I see.' The manager gave a slow grin. 'Your job depends on it, you might say? All right, I'll help you, but you'll have to give me a receipt. First of all I'd like some proof, too, that you are from the Cosy Cinema.'

'That's easy,' Sid said, fully prepared, and he handed across his union card for the N.A.T.K.E. Bennet studied it.

'Right: that's enough for me.' He handed the card back. 'Have to make sure, you know. I've only one fear — that the film may have been returned to the stock department for scrap. Just a moment.'

Sid waited, far more anxious than he appeared. His hopes rose and fell by turns as Bennet contacted department after department in the inner recesses of the big building — then at last, after nearly ten minutes of inquiry, a circular film can was brought in by a man in a baize apron.

'Got it!' Bennet exclaimed in triumph, wrenching off the lid. 'This is it, I think.'

Sid got to his feet, watching intently as Bennet pulled aside the purple protective paper. A strong odour of pear drops rose as he raised the five-hundred foot length and unravelled the start.

'This is it all right,' he confirmed. 'And here's the examiner's tag. See . . . '

Sid picked up the tag-label and read: *Examined by A.J. Sound Track useless owing to severe scratching. Scrap.*

'How long can I keep it?' Sid asked. 'I've no idea how long it will take me to get to the root of the trouble.'

'Long as you like, provided we *do* get it back. Let's say, provisonally, a month. If you're no nearer by then let us know and we'll extend the time. We have to account for everything to the exhibitors, remember. I'll have a receipt made out for you to sign, and this film had better go in a transit case. I don't have to tell you that the law won't let you carry it around otherwise.'

Sid nodded and said nothing. He was feeling a warm glow of satisfaction at having accomplished his object. A few minutes later he signed the receipt and then left the building with the small transit case in his hand. At a nearby restaurant he stopped and had lunch.

10

Many a slip

Sid caught the 2-50 out of London and was entering his home again at four o'clock. He greeted his mother — who was under the impression that he had been to London on behalf of the cinema to get a much-needed film in a hurry — and then he went out into the woodshed where he did most of his tinkering. Here he unravelled the film before the light of the window and studied it through a pocket lens.

The scratchings on the sound track were so plainly visible that they made him whistle in amazement. No wonder the renters had raised hell! In fact they were more than scratches — the entire emulsion had been scraped away from the celluloid base, much the same way as paint blisters away from wood under heat.

Sid went doggedly from one end of the

reel to the other, coming very early on the joint which Billy had made to repair the break caused by Terry. Otherwise there was not a joint in the whole length of the film. But from end to end the persistence of track damage was absolute — yet it never moved over the edge of the sound track on to the picture itself. 'Which can only mean it was done as it ran,' Sid mused, his eyes narrowed in thought. 'Otherwise the scratching could never have been so confined to this eighth-of-an-inch track. Looks to me as though it was done with the point of a pin, or needle. Of all the damned queer things! I don't see either sense or reason in such deliberate mutilation. I'll swear by everything I've got that there was nothing in the track, before it was ruined, that could have caused vibration. There was only Fitzpatrick's voice and a bit of background music here and there.'

He put the film down and strolled outside to smoke a cigarette and think the business out. Very strange. He had smoked the cigarette down to the stub without coming any nearer to a solution.

Returning to the film he examined it again. He could see the equidistant dots on the sprocket-hole side of the track, but thought nothing of them. They were probably 'emulsion bubbles' and nothing more — a common fault in a film and often the cause of sprocket hum. Slowly he wound the film back to the beginning and sighed to himself.

'At least I can hear what it sounds like,' he promised himself finally, and from a shelf he dragged out an amateur amplifier and sound-reproducer which he had built for himself at odd times. He fitted the film on to a spool and laced it through the rather rickety but quite efficient sound-gate. Then he switched on the motor and listened to the reproduction.

He had never heard anything to equal it. All the noises of a battlefield, mixed with jet planes, motor cycle exhausts, and falling bombs were all jumbled together with the announcer's voice somewhere in the background.

'Wow!' Sid gasped, hastily switching off. 'Ruined is right! It's enough to wreck my photoelectric cell . . . ' and he looked at it anxiously, to find that, fortunately, it had not been damaged.

He was beaten. He sat down on the stool and stared at the film intently, turning over a variety of possibilities in his mind, but none of them seemed to lead anywhere. By no possible stretch of imagination or mechanics did there seem to be anything about the film that could bring down a globe.

'Wonder if I'm crazy?' he muttered. 'If all this is just a mad coincidence? Maybe I've been imagining all sorts of things. Perhaps the globe did come down by accident. Perhaps Terry did only snatch at the film in a moment of panic, just as we all do at times . . . ' Sid shook his head. 'No! Too many 'perhaps's about it. And there *was* that design in the dust on top of the still-case . . . wait a minute! I wonder! I wonder if I ran this film again if the same design would appear again?'

The idea took a hold on him and then clouded before another thought.

'I don't quite see that it would be much use trying. The track wasn't in this awful mess that time. It was apparently quite normal. This row would make a design in a chunk of granite, I should think . . . ' He pondered for a moment. 'Or *would* it? Perhaps it wouldn't. It's only a *noise*, and that's very different from a pure vibration. Most pure vibrations can't *be* heard, come to think of it. Hell fire, what am I getting into? Looks as if I'm nose-diving into ultrasonics.'

He thought a bit further, chiefly upon the textbook he had read on designs.

'Fine sand or powder, plate glass, supported underneath in the centre,' he murmured. 'Okay. There's no reason why I can't do that right here.'

He got up from the stool and began rummaging amidst the pile of odds and ends that he had in different parts of the shed, finally unearthing the glass out of an old picture frame. To find an upright block of wood and some glue was not a long job. He did not wait for the glue to set. He was satisfied that the glass would stay in place from sheer tackiness.

This done, he went into the house, borrowed the cocoa tin from his mother — to her complete astonishment — and covered the top of the glass sheet with the fine powder. It was the nearest substitute he could find for sand at the moment and ought to be every bit as satisfactory.

He placed the plate at a distance of about three feet from the reproducer's loudspeaker, re-threaded the film, and then started it off again. He stood wincing at the noise — then he forgot all about the din as he studied the amazing convulsions taking place in the cocoa powder. In a direct line with the speaker, the powder was assuming all kinds of fantastic shapes, spilling powder over the edge of the plate — forming into stars, circles, triangles, and then such complicated, snaky patterns that Sid lost track altogether.

Finally he switched off, and the silence was a profound relief.

'Those crackles and bangs didn't do that!' he told himself flatly. 'Like hell they did! There's something else in this film — there *must* be, and I haven't found yet what it is.'

Yet again he examined it, and yet again he passed over the dots as emulsion bubbles and nothing more. Looking for something really significant, the very minuteness of the explanation escaped him. His big face was grim as he wound the film up at last and dumped it back in the can.

'Only one way out of this! I'll try it on the same machine it ran on before. I'll get some fine sand from one of the fire buckets and spread it on the still-case top. Then I'll run the darned thing and see if anything happens in the cinema where the power amplifiers have more strength.' He thought for a moment. 'Mmm, easy to talk. How do I do it? I can't let Terry know anything, and I can't do it on his day off tomorrow with Billy there and the cleaners at work. Nor do I want to stay behind at night on the pretext of doing some repair work. That'd look far too suspicious, and Terry would think things. But I have got to have the cinema to myself after a night show — and since I've no passkey that isn't going to be easy. To break in isn't practicable, either . . . '

For a while the problem really had him worried — then he grinned triumphantly as a natural solution presented itself. On Wednesday night the transport men would be coming at midnight as usual with a new load of film. The men had a key with which to enter the cinema. He could quite easily conceal himself in the shadows outside the cinema entrance — he knew the best spot — and, when the door opened, he could slip in and keep quiet until the coast was clear. He would be locked in the building to do as he wished, to leave later by an emergency exit, which would shut itself by simply pulling the doors to. He could tell his mother there was more late work to be done on the houselights and she would never question the fact.

As for the film — to carry it there without it being seen, he would have to wrap it round and round his body and cement the end into place to keep it from unravelling.

'I'll do it,' he told himself. 'Hanged if I won't. Then we'll see if anything happens.'

★ ★ ★

As Terry came down the Circle staircase after the show that evening, Billy beside him, he saw Helen Prescott's graceful figure strolling about the foyer. She was wearing a light coat, which he had never seen before, and an exceedingly fetching hat was perched on her glossy dark hair.

'Wow!' Billy murmured, studying her as he descended the stairs. 'Looks like our little Hel got a raise for herself. Nice piece, Terry — let's face it.'

Terry lighted a cigarette and said nothing. He and Billy came to the base of the stairs and Billy gave a wide grin.

'Waiting for a street car, sweetheart?' he enquired.

Helen gave him a look. 'Supposing I am? What do you propose doing about it?'

'Nothing. Only don't mind me saying that Terry's a sucker to let you slip the way he has. I could even fall for you myself only I like 'em blonde, and much plumper . . . Well, see you tomorrow.'

'Not me you won't,' Terry said. 'It's my day off.'

'Blimey, so it is. I'll have to put up with

the apeman all day!'

Billy went and the spring doors closed silently behind him. Terry came to a stop and looked at Helen critically. He raised one eyebrow in cynical amusement.

'It goes without saying, of course, that this getup isn't for my edification?' he asked.

'Yes, it goes without saying,' Helen agreed. 'We don't have to go into all that again, do we? Matter of fact, I'm waiting for Mark.'

'Mark?' Terry gave a frown.

'Mr. Turner,' Helen explained deliberately, holding out her left hand. On the third finger was a circlet of gold with two glittering diamonds clawed thereon.

'I see,' Terry commented grimly. 'So things have got that far!'

'Exactly!'

Terry put his cigarette back in his mouth and reflected.

'Funny thing,' he said slowly. 'Five minutes — less even — and you'd not be wearing that ring . . . '

'Five minutes?' Helen's eyes were frankly puzzled. 'What are you talking about? *What* five minutes?'

'I'm thinking about Vera Holdsworth. Remember how that globe fell on her? You were there just before she got hit, weren't you? You'd be pushing up daises now instead of her, but for that five minutes.'

'But I'm *not* pushing up daisies! I'm alive, and enjoying it! The thought that I just missed what Vera got did scare me at the time, but I've got over it now.'

Terry looked at her, his colour deepening. 'Yes, you've got over it, because I saved your life! That's what it amounts to! You never thought of — '

He stopped, tightened his mouth, then without another word he strode through the foyer swing doors and was gone. Helen remained motionless, his words still in her mind.

''Because I saved your life',' she repeated, half aloud. 'Now what *did* he mean by that?'

'What did who mean by what?' Mark Turner asked, coming over to her after locking his office door. 'What's the matter, Helen?'

'I — I've just been talking to Terry.'

'Oh? Did you show him the engagement ring?' Turner failed to keep jealous satisfaction out of his voice.

'Yes . . . ' Helen said slowly. 'I showed it to him.'

'And did you tell him that you're going to become my private secretary instead of chief usherette, until we're married?'

'No. I didn't have the time. Matter of fact, Mark, I was trying to puzzle out something he said to me. Something impulsive and angry — something he bit off at the end as though he'd never intended to say it.'

Turner said nothing. He led Helen through the main doors, locked them, and then they went down the steps together.

'What did he say?' he asked presently.

'He was remarking that had I been on the seat where Vera sat, in the Circle, when that houselight fell, I wouldn't be here now as your future wife. He flared up and said I was only here because he had saved my life . . . Don't you see, Mark?' Helen went on, her voice quickening, 'he couldn't have known he *was* going to save my life unless he had known beforehand that Vera was going to be killed!'

Turner reflected for a while, then, 'You're *sure* he said just that?'

'Absolutely sure! It's a horrible thought — *horrible*! Unless I got the wrong slant on it. You do see, Mark, don't you?'

'Yes — I see. Stating it bluntly, it sounds as though he deliberately arranged the accident that caused the death of Vera.'

'Yes . . . ' Helen frowned. 'I must have misunderstood. He'd never do a thing like that. It's too appalling a thing to even contemplate!'

'Helen, there is something you ought to know about.' Turner's voice showed he had made up his mind about something. 'I can tell you about it now because we mean so much to each other . . . You remember the burglary, the two hundred and five pounds which was stolen? Terry was the thief.'

Helen came to a stop. '*Terry* was?'

'Superintendent Standish proved it to the hilt, but there was nothing we could do — no evidence on which we could charge Terry. I was in the position — and still am — of knowing the facts and yet being unable to do anything about them. I decided that Terry must have been desperate, and let it go at that. Because I knew him to be a thief I did all in my power to stop you associating with him — coupled, of course, with the fact that I wanted you for myself.'

'Now I understand something,' Helen said slowly. 'There's always been something in his nature that I couldn't fathom — a barrier of some sort. I've sensed that he has a deceitful streak somewhere. Mother was even more candid: she says she can't bear the sight of him.'

They came to the corner of the street where Helen's home stood.

'I'm thinking of something Superintendent Standish said to me when we agreed we should keep an eye on Terry,' Turner resumed presently. 'He said that once a chap starts going on the wrong track he has a habit of getting deeper in. One thing leads to another . . . And, judging from what Terry said to you in an impulsive moment, he *has* got deeper in. *Much* deeper in.'

'Honesty, Mark, I still can't believe that he'd try to kill Vera. He couldn't have done because he was in the projection room when the globe fell. Besides, even though he had quarrelled with Vera he surely wouldn't want to kill her just on *that* score. He wouldn't be such an idiot.'

Turner halted outside the gateway of Helen's home.

'Before we go in, let's agree how we stand. We haven't an atom of proof that he committed that burglary. And even if he deliberately arranged the death of Vera, we can also be sure he's kept himself without suspicion. Right now, we can't do a thing.'

'But I've told you what he said to me. He *knew* Vera was going to be killed, or at any rate smashed up. We ought to tell the police — '

'It wouldn't do any good, dear. They wouldn't even listen. You had no witness with you who also heard what he said. There's nothing we can do — except get rid of him from the cinema at the earliest moment. I'm placing a lot of advertise-ments as it is, and have been ever since I found he was a thief. Unfortunately I can't just throw him out: without a chief projectionist I'll be in a spot.'

'He's a murderer,' Helen whispered.

'We don't know he is,' Turner insisted. 'Circumstantial evidence can be deadly sometimes. We've got to apparently forget it for the moment. And remember, not a word of what we suspect. It might even put you in danger. Whether Terry realizes the mistake he's made, or not, we don't know, but I imagine he's smart enough to guess that nothing can be done without a witness. Someday things will catch up on him — and by that time I hope he's no longer in my employ. From now on I'll shift heaven and earth to get rid of him.'

⋆   ⋆   ⋆

Sid arrived at the cinema the following morning to find everything apparently normal. There was the stale smell of the morning after; the doorman cracking doubtful jokes; the usherettes with their dusters; and Billy as impudent as ever. In fact there seemed to be only one change in the humdrum procedure, and Sid discovered it in mid-morning when the need for some blank slides took him to Mark Turner's office. He tried not to look surprised at finding Helen there, laboriously typing out letters with Turner seated at the other end of the roll-top desk.

'Morning, Sid,' Turner greeted genially. 'Something wanted?'

'Er — yes.' Sid rubbed the back of his untidy head and glanced at Helen. 'Just some blank slides, please.'

Turner handed some over from a cubbyhole on his desk, and then he said, 'Helen is my secretary, pro tem, Sid — and Kathleen Gatty will become head usherette. I'll be getting some more usherettes soon, I hope . . . Helen and I are going to be married. No reason why you shouldn't know about it.'

Sid's big, plain face lighted in genuine pleasure. 'You are? Well, that's fine! I'm really glad, sir — and for you, Helen. Is it in order to shake hands and congratulate you both?'

Turner laughed. 'Of course!'

Sid's big red paw came forth and he shook hands vigorously. Then he caught a thoughtful glance from Turner.

'Sid, there's something I've been meaning to ask you. What repairs did Terry make to the projector on those two nights he stayed behind?'

The question caught Sid off balance, and as usual he betrayed the fact. He looked definitely uncomfortable.

'It's some little time ago now, sir. I hardly remember.'

'You must try to. You see, I'm paying a bill for fifty two pounds odd for a ruined Fitzpatrick film. I told Terry about it at the time and he said he thought he'd cured the fault on the machine that caused the trouble. The sound track was scratched from end to end.'

'Was it?' Sid asked vaguely.

'It was.' Turner looked at him steadily. 'What I can't understand is why Terry spent two nights — for what period of time I don't know — making the machine right and then a fault turns up, which ruins the sound track and costs me fifty pounds! I'm asking you for your opinion

282

because you're a good technician. What could *cause* the track to be ruined in that way?'

'As far as I can see, nothing,' Sid answered. 'That is, I'd say that off hand. I'd have to look to make sure. I'll do that if you like — but we haven't been having any trouble lately.'

'And there wasn't any trouble before, either. All the upset seemed to be centred on that Travelogue film.'

'I — I didn't know there was anything wrong with it,' Sid said, reddening a little.

'There was — a good deal.' Turner sat back in his chair. 'I have been having a word with Cliff Dixon, the service engineer, this morning. My own lack of technical knowledge doesn't signify when I have him to call on.'

Sid was silent — and alarmed. Clifford Dixon, the service engineer, knew all there was to know about projectors and sound equipment, and a good deal more besides.

'He tells me,' Turner continued, 'that a film which sounded perfect in the hall could not become severely scratched afterwards — unless it were caused *deliberately*. He assures me that there is no fixture or sprocket on the machine which could ruin a film in the manner that Travelogue was ruined.'

Sid looked at Helen, at the desk, and then rubbed his neck.

'You know that Dixon is right, don't you?' Turner asked.

'Yes, sir — he's right. But I didn't have anything to do with damaging the film.'

'I'm sure of that. Dixon says that a film could only have been ruined in that way by deliberately scratching it as it ran through the projector below the sound gate. You were not running that particular machine at the time, so obviously you had nothing to do with it.'

'You mean, sir, that you think *Terry* ruined it? That it?'

Turner did not answer the question. 'Listen, Sid. Terry damaged his fingers pretty badly in snatching at that Travelogue, didn't he? It looks to me as though he broke the film on purpose. I'd like to know exactly what did happen.'

Sid thought for a moment, then: 'To get the timing absolutely accurate, sir, he snatched at the film just after I had remarked that you, Helen, were seated on the tip-up instead of Vera, who usually was seated there.'

'Then what happened?' Turner asked quietly.

'Well, I — Terry's hand was in such a mess I laced the film up for him and I was going to run it, but instead he elbowed me out of the way and said he'd do it himself . . . Frankly, sir, I don't quite see what you're getting at.'

'You wouldn't prefer to be absolutely frank with me, Sid, would you?'

'Frank? About what?' Sid began to bluster. 'I don't know anything about that film! Honest I don't! You've just admitted that fact yourself, and — '

Sid stopped. Turner had picked up a letter from his desk. Without a word he handed it over. Sid read it, a frown creeping onto his forehead. It was from the Zenith Film Distributors and marked 'Confidential.'

Dear Mr. Turner,

In confidence, your second projectionist, Mr. Sidney Elbridge, called here yesterday with a request to borrow the Fitzpatrick Travelogue recently damaged by one of your projectors. He said he wished to test it to find out the cause of the trouble. He also said that the defect was probably his responsibility, and on that account he would be glad if I would repress all information. Nevertheless, as manager, I think you should know the peculiar circumstances.

Truly yours,
  Arthur Bennet

'Oh, Lord!' Sid muttered, and handed the letter back.

'You admit it, then?' Turner asked.

'Yes, sir, I admit it. I have the film at home now — but I *didn't* ruin it. And I had nothing to do with it. I only said that to Mr. Bennet because I couldn't think of any other way to keep the business private.'

Turner nodded. 'All right, I believe you. But how did you know the film had been damaged? Since I never mentioned it I assume it was Terry who told you?'

'No. That day when I came down here for a slide I saw the letter on your desk referring to the damage. I read it, hardly meaning to, while you were telephoning.'

'Mmmm. And what do you want the film for, anyway? What do you hope to do about it?'

The placid atmosphere was too much for Sid. Suddenly he brought his fist down on the desk vehemently.

'Think what you like — fire me out on my ear if you want to — but I believe Vera Holdsworth was *murdered*! I believe it was *Terry* who murdered her, and I further believe that the Travelogue film was somehow responsible for it.' Sid stopped and rubbed the back of his thick neck. 'Well, there it is. I've said it. When do I quit?'

Turner got to his feet and gripped Sid's powerful arm.

'You don't quit, Sid: you stay. You stay until you've got to the bottom of this business. I thought you'd tell me everything of your own volition, but I had to prompt you into it . . . You believe Vera

Holdsworth was murdered. All right, so do I! And so, too, does Helen.'

Helen nodded slowly as Sid glanced in her direction. Then he looked back at the manager.

'You *do*? But what evidence have you got, sir?'

'None that will hold water. What about you?'

'Lots of things!' Sid snapped. 'I've worked mighty hard to scrape facts together. I got my first clue by a technical — '

'That's the point,' Turner interrupted. 'You're a good technician, Sid, and this murder — if murder it was — was technically brilliant. I can't call in the police on flimsy evidence, therefore the whole onus relies on you. If you can solve how it was done, let me know. I thought, however, that you should know where I stand, and Helen too.'

Sid was silent for a long time, then he looked at Turner seriously.

'Well, sir, I've got plans — and I want to work them out in my own way. I can so handle things that Terry will never suspect what I'm up to.'

'Then, go to it,' Turner said promptly. 'I don't want to know what you're doing, and I probably wouldn't understand one half of it if you told me. Go right ahead.'

'You mean I have your full support in everything?'

'You have the support of both of us. You don't think I'm going to put anything in the way of you proving murder, do you?'

'I'll go on to the bitter end,' Sid vowed. 'Vera meant a great deal to me, and I don't care how long I work or how complicated a job it is, just as long as I finally prove she was cold-bloodedly murdered . . .' Sid paused, reflected, then seemed to come to a decision. 'I believe, sir, it was Terry who burgled this office — in spite of the fact that the case seems to have been dropped.'

Turner smiled a little. 'You're right, Sid: Terry was the thief. Even the police know that, but there's no proof.'

'I'm glad to know that I was right,' Sid muttered. 'What is more, I know *why* he burgled. It probably looked as though he did it to pay his bookie — but there was another reason. He was afraid, I think, that you might question him as to where he had obtained two hundred pounds to bet *with*. I can tell you where he got it, and about another hundred pounds as well. He's been using plant equipment, intended for replacements, and converting it to use for sub-standard projectors, which he sells to amateurs for a good profit.'

Turner's expression changed. 'He has, eh? Consistent theft, you mean?'

'That's about the size of it. Going back some three years.'

'Is there enough evidence to make a charge against him?'

'I don't know enough about the law to say, sir — but he'd certainly have a hard time explaining where everything has gone if you decided to tackle him about it. Unless, of course, he has the stuff at home and could replace it; but I hardly think that is the case . . . As far as I'm concerned I'm more interested in finding out by what method he brought the houselight down on Vera. What thieving he has done is trivial beside that.'

'Yes, Sid, you're right. If I were to charge him with theft he'd be wary of never saying a word that might convict him of murder. On the other hand, if we let him be and don't show him that we think anything is wrong he might, in the presence of witnesses, say something to give himself away. As he did last night to Helen.'

'He did?' Sid repeated.

Turner related what had occurred. Sid stood thinking, a gleam in his eyes.

'Couldn't be anything more conclusive than that,' he said finally. 'He *did* do it. The one thing now is to try and find out *how*.'

'Exactly,' Turner agreed. 'I'd thought of having a shot at it myself, which is why I tackled Cliff Dixon. Then, from some of the things Helen told me I realized that you might already be trying to do something about the business. Since you are, and are a trained technician, I'll retire and see what happens.'

'I'm stuck for motive, as a matter of fact,' Sid confessed. 'I can't think why Terry committed the crime. Eliminating every other angle I can only think that perhaps Vera *caught* him stealing and that she held it over his head. So he had to get rid of her. That would make the whole thing logical. She did come back to the cinema on the night of the burglary, because her parents told me as much . . . or at any rate her mother told me.'

'If she did come back,' Helen said, 'it would probably be for her cigarettes.'

Sid and Turner looked at her in surprise.

'How did you know?' Sid asked.

'She told me to remind her to take her cigarettes out of her uniform pocket when the show was over. I forgot all about it. If she came back I'll bet it was to get them. She smoked like a flue remember, and she had a passkey to the building, too.'

'That satisfies me!' Sid said, clenching his fist. 'At first, when I knew Vera had come back here, I got the impression that she had perhaps committed the theft herself, then it occurred to me she would never have told her parents she was coming back here if she intended robbing the place. Since she told you about the cigarettes as well, Helen, we can be pretty sure that she came back solely for that reason, and caught Terry on the job.'

'I suppose,' Helen said thoughtfully, 'there isn't any way of tricking Terry into a confession? Or at least a statement?'

Sid shook his head. 'Not a chance! He's too wary — but this I do know: once I have all the facts I'll make him talk. Don't worry about that.'

'Then I think we can leave it at that,' Turner said quietly. 'Go ahead, Sid, and do what you can. If you need any help at all I will — '

'As a matter of fact, I *do* need help. I was going to slide into the building tomorrow night when the transport men come, since I've got no key — but if you can let me have a key I'll return tonight and try my experiment.'

'Experiment?'

'An experiment with the Travelogue film. It'll be highly technical, but maybe you'd like to watch me and see what I'm driving at?'

'You bet I would!' Turner exclaimed.

'Tonight all three of us will leave in the ordinary way, so the rest of the staff will not be in any way suspicious. We'll have supper in town, then you and I, Sid, will come back here.'

11

Demonstration

Now that he had Mark Turner and Helen on his side, and knew that as far as they were concerned secrecy was no longer necessary, Sid felt vastly relieved. He was even cheerful throughout the rest of the day and proved it by ragging young Billy unmercifully.

That evening, Sid closed down in the ordinary way and left the cinema ahead of Helen and Turner, waiting for them outside. After about ten minutes, when the rest of the staff had departed, they joined him under the street lamps.

'Everything prepared, Sid?' Turner questioned.

'Yes, sir. Nobody knows a thing about the intended experiment, except you and Helen.'

Turner nodded. 'Let's get along and have some supper. We may have a long night before us.'

'I wish I could watch the experiment too,' Helen said regretfully. 'But I suppose it would hardly do to land home about three in the morning and be unable to explain myself.'

'Hardly,' Turner agreed. 'But you're going to have supper with us. On that I'm determined.'

He carried his intention through and towards 11-15 he saw Helen to her home, stayed for a few moments, and then returned to the corner of the street where Sid was waiting for him . . . Together they re-entered the cinema's dark, warm expanse.

'I have the feeling, sir,' Sid said, as they went up the black abyss of staircase, 'that we're dealing with something which is a problem in sound — ultrasonics, in fact. Which is just the sort of smart idea that Terry would think of. I got the notion first when I found a design in the dust on top of that still-frame I'm fixing in the Circle.'

'Design in the dust?' Turner repeated, puzzled — then he gave himself up to listening as Sid explained in detail what he had discovered so far. By the time he had finished, he and Turner were together in the brightly lighted winding room, and Sid was stripping off his shirt. Turner watched him uncoil the film wrapped round and round his body over his singlet.

'So we're getting into ultrasonics, eh?' Turner mused. 'And you've tested this film at home on your own apparatus and got designs in cocoa powder? Well, what does that prove?'

'As I tell you, sir, I'm stumped,' Sid confessed. 'I know the film causes the weird designs, but I don't know why . . . I've examined it, and I can't find the reason. It isn't the scratching itself: it's something else. That's why I want to see what happens — if anything — when I run it on the ordinary projector and sound apparatus.'

He finished the job of spooling the film, put his shirt on again, and then led the way up the steps to the projection room. To thread the film on to No. 1 machine was only the work of a moment. Turner lounged against the amplifier rack, watching interestedly. Very rarely did he come into this region of machines and electricity. He moved presently and stared through the portholes into the blank darkness of the hall.

'So far, so good,' Sid announced. 'Now I want some sand to put on top of the still case. We'll want the cleaning light on too, so I'll — '

'I'll fix it,' Turner said, and hurried off down the steps.

He met Sid again in the Circle as Sid brought the ladder and propped it against the wall. A heavy sand-bucket in his hand Sid ascended the ladder and carefully covered the top of the still case with fine sand. Then he descended again and gave a nod.

'If you'll wait here, sir, I'll come back and join you,' he said. 'Then we'll see what happens.'

Turner lighted a cigarette and settled himself on the back row of the Circle, the wall of which was the outer wall of the projection room. He glanced about him thoughtfully. The amber satin curtains swept back from the screen and Fitz-patrick's Travelogue came into view with its 'Voice of the Globe' title. Turner began to wince at the appalling noise that roared from the speakers, blotting out the normal overture music.

Sid returned again, lighted a Turkish, and settled at Turner's side.

'I put the arc on, sir, so we can see it as well,' Sid explained. 'I remember the approximate time when the globe fell. Picture of a bay, I think it was.'

'The arc will be all right, I suppose? Won't the carbons burn down?'

'Automatic feed is on, sir. The light will be all right.'

They both sat listening to the awful cacophony. Not a single word of the commentary was intelligible, and the amplified concussions smote up here with an almost physical force.

'This is bad enough to bring down the whole cinema, never mind a houselight,' Turner commented at length. 'I don't see that we're proving anything, either. This noise wasn't going on when the house-light fell.'

'Of itself, the noise means nothing, and *does* nothing,' Sid answered. 'It is caused by the extreme variations of light striking the photo-electric cell as the scratches pass over it in varying thickness and designs. There! Hear that bump? That is the joint Billy made after Terry snapped the film . . . Now it was a little after this point that the trouble started. I want to see if it's possible to get through this film without anything unusual happening. If the design is again reproduced in the sand up there on the still case, I — '

Sid broke off and jerked his face upwards. Turner did the same. To both of them there had come the distinct sound of splintering glass. They were just in time to see the two big new houselight bulbs nearest to them, at the very back of the Circle, splinter into a mass of fragments and leave bare filaments.

Sid leapt up. 'See that?' he demanded. 'Did you see it?'

Turner was looking mystified. 'Of course I saw it! Two lamps gone west!'

'It means something much more exciting than that, sir.' Sid stubbed out his cigarette and raced out of the Circle.

After a moment or two the shattering

din from the screen speakers ceased and the picture vanished. Sid returned at a run. Without looking at Turner, who was contemplating the two shattered house-light bulbs, he hurried across to the ladder against the wall and climbed the rungs swiftly.

'We've got it, sir!' he shouted. 'Exactly the same design again! Come and look!'

Turner hurried to the ladder, mounted it, and standing two rungs below Sid he gazed at the incredible intricacy of the design that had been traced in the sand.

'Yes, that looks like it right enough,' he admitted. 'But I must say I'm utterly at sea.'

He climbed down the ladder again and stood pondering as Sid got busy with the fire bucket, swept the sand from the top of the case back into it, and then descended to the floor. He returned the bucket to its normal position and then looked up at the shattered bulbs.

'There's no doubt any more, sir, that we're dealing with ultrasonics,' he commented. 'Inaudible sound in the form of pure vibration.'

'Inaudible!' Turner echoed. 'But that infernal row we've been listening to would wake the dead!'

'That had nothing to do with it,' Sid insisted. 'That is what I meant when I said the noise counted for nothing. You see, an ultrasonic wave is in a different class to plain noise. It operates far above normal sound, and for that reason normal sound cannot affect it.'

'Oh!' Turner was baffled, but tried not to show it.

Sid went on, 'Another thing is pretty obvious, too. At the height where these houselights hang — and above them, which includes the top of the still-case — an ultrasonic wave was going full blast whilst that Travelogue was running. It comes from the screen speakers. It affected those two hanging bulbs we fitted recently and smashed their glass to bits — just the kind of glass that *would* smash too under ultrasonic vibration.'

'Maybe, but only *one* houselight came down — the one which killed Vera,' Turner pointed out. 'The one on the left here — and then it wasn't the whole globe. Only the lower hemisphere.'

'Yes . . . ' Sid thought for a moment. 'And that hemisphere must have dropped in *one piece*, not in fragments, otherwise it would not have hit Vera with the terrific force intended. It broke when it *did* hit her, of course, but that isn't the point. The twin houselight on the right wasn't affected, even though it must have been in the range of the vibration. In any case, I don't think a supersonic wave would have been able to smash those opal globes. They're thick and solid, just a bulb has glass which is thin and brittle.'

'Certainly that lower hemisphere came down in one piece,' Turner said. 'Witnesses at the inquest testified to the fact. The assumption was that the screws had contracted too much owing to the ventilator draught, or something. Remember?'

'Yes . . . Yes, I remember.'

Turner fondled his chin. 'How in the name of sanity does that Travelogue *produce* an ultrasonic vibration? Is it by accident, a flaw in the recording, or what?'

'It can't be a flaw in the recording, sir, otherwise it would not have been necessary for Terry to ruin the track afterwards. He did that with the obvious intention of making the film useless, so it would be converted into scrap and destroy the evidence. The fact remains that an ultrasonic vibration *is* produced, but I can't fathom how.'

'To me,' Turner said presently, 'there is another problem just as big. How did an ultrasonic wave bring down the lower hemisphere of that globe? It couldn't, could it?'

'The original fixture is in the winding room — where we put all of them after we'd taken them down. We might do worse than take a look at them.'

Turner nodded and followed Sid upstairs. From a corner of the winding room Sid finally dragged out the massive old fixture they wanted. It was a complete globe, for after the accident a spare lower hemisphere opal had been fitted — the one indeed with which Terry had originally experimented — until the new houselight fixtures had arrived. The fact that the opal was slightly duller in texture than all the others made it easily identifiable . . . In the bright light Sid examined the turnscrews, turning them back and forth on their threads with Turner watching over his shoulder.

'They're mighty slack,' Sid commented, frowning. 'A mere touch moves them along the threads. First time I've thought of examining them. Terry himself took care to fit a new hemisphere so I didn't have the chance to spot anything. Not that I had any suspicions at the time, anyway.'

From the corner he hauled up two more of the globes and tested the screws. By comparison they were stiff. Grimness slowly settled on Turner's face.

'It looks to me,' he said, 'as though the screws on that particular lamp have been turned back and forth so that they move without difficulty. The experts must have noticed that also, but evidently they didn't attach much importance to it.'

'Probably because they didn't compare them with the tightness of the screws on the *other* lamps,' Sid said. 'I'll tell you what I think we should do, even though it may take a bit of time. The winches and cables are still in place in the false roof. I think I'll haul this lamp back in position with the screw points only just holding the hemisphere in place. Then I'll run the Travelogue again and see what happens.'

'Right! I'll help you.'

Turner pulled off his raincoat and the jacket of his evening suit, then he and Sid got busy . . . In fifteen minutes they were in the Circle again, watching the hanging globe earnestly as the noisy film was run through, without vision, from the grey screen. Almost after the same period as before, when the bulbs had broken, the lower hemisphere abruptly detached itself from its screw fittings and dropped downwards. It struck the floor immediately beneath the tip-up seat, bounced, and rolled to a standstill on the thick carpet.

Turner sat in silence for a moment; then he looked at Sid.

'That's *it*!' Sid muttered. 'We've got the answer! The screws were loosened beforehand by Terry — to the danger point — and as long as no supersonic vibration took place the globe was okay. He knew that. The Travelogue film he 'prepared' in some way to make it produce the inaudible vibration. He was all set, then when I noticed that Helen and not Vera was on the tip-up seat he tried to stop the show, or at least delay it, by snapping the film. I insisted that he carry on. He did so because Vera had come back. After a while the inaudible vibration shifted the screws back along the grooves and . . . '

Turner stared at the globe hemisphere on the carpet. He seemed incapable of saying anything. Sid went on talking, recapitulating pensively.

'On the two nights he supposedly fixed his machine he was probably making tests. He must have doctored the film on the Friday night after it had had its evening run. He knew there would only be a kids' matinee on Saturday afternoon, so the Travelogue would not be used until the Saturday night, when the trouble happened. After that, the film would be taken away and, he hoped, destroyed because of its condition.'

'It seems incredible,' Turner whispered. 'No one but a madman would think up such a fiendish idea!'

'I found a sliver of glass, too,' Sid added presently. 'I think it came from a tumbler missing from the washroom. I'll bet he used it to test whereabouts the ultrasonic vibration was striking. He overlooked one thing, however: ultrasonic vibrations make patterns, and that one in the dust on the still-case started me off, together with the fact that two screws had been mysteriously pushed from one end of the case top to the other . . . Yes, we know *how* he did it, but we still have to find out what he did to that film.'

'Let's have another look at it,' Turner said curtly.

They went back upstairs and Sid removed the film from the projector after switching the machine off. Without a word he went down into the winding room with Turner behind him. Tossing the free end of the film on to an empty spool Sid fixed the loaded spool on the opposite winder. The film lay bright and clear under the strong electric light.

'You can see the markings quite distinctly,' Sid said, handing Turner his pocket lens. 'Take a look.'

Turner bent over the film, winding it slowly from one spool to the other. After a long study he straightened up and frowned.

'Yes, the scratchings are plain enough,' he agreed, 'but what about those little pin holes at the side? Very, very tiny, like dots. That normal?'

'No, not exactly. Emulsion bubbles that haven't dried out properly in the printing. We often get them and they sometimes cause a hum in the sound gate. In this case that didn't happen because, before the film was ruined, there was no trace of hum.'

'Emulsion. Bubbles . . . ' Turner repeated slowly. 'In that case you mean that the emulsion has settled in minute bubbles?'

'Right.'

'But surely they would be on the emulsion side of the film? These dots go right *through* the film. They're holes!'

Sid's expression changed. 'Holes? Holes?

Here, let me see!'

He nearly snatched the lens from Turner's fingers and peered at the film earnestly, edging it along inch by inch. Finally he lowered his hands and stared fixedly in front of him.

'You're right, sir — dead right!' he breathed. 'When I examined this film at home the light wasn't too good: there's a tree, which keeps the light off the woodshed where I do most of my tinkering. When I saw the dots I assumed they were emulsion bubbles. I got no bright edgewise light on the reverse side, as I have now, otherwise I'd have seen these holes . . . Hell, but this makes a world of difference! No film ever got like this in the ordinary way. These holes are as deliberate as the scratching of the sound track.'

Sid frowned and put the lens back in his pocket. 'Even now I don't see how it could produce an ultrasonic vibration. Seems to me there would be just a high-pitched hum and nothing more. Unless the speed of the film's transit has something to do with it. In the matter of

310

sound mechanics Terry has a far greater knowledge than I.'

'So it seems,' Turner commented bitterly. 'Of all the devilish ideas, this about takes the biscuit — '

'Tell you what!' Sid snapped his fingers suddenly. 'There's one man who can make rings round Terry when it comes to sound mechanics, and that's Cliff Dixon, our service engineer. What is more, he has all kinds of instruments for testing, which we haven't got.'

'Yes, you're right there,' Turner made the admission slowly, as he reflected. 'He might be able to give us the answer, but he wouldn't be human if he didn't want to know the reason. What do we tell him?'

'The truth. We're battening down on a murderer, so why should we hide anything? Cliff's a reasonable chap: he'll keep his mouth shut if we ask him to.'

Turner glanced at his watch. 'Half past twelve. He's used to being called on emergencies, so I'll see if I can get him. I'll make the excuse that we have sound trouble and are working late. I'll go and give him a ring.'

Sid nodded and began to rewind the film back to the start. He took it upstairs and relaced it into the projector. Then he stood with his fists clenched.

'Filthy, murdering devil,' he whispered. 'I'll get him for this if it's the last thing I do! The law will hang him, but not before I've put in my two cents' worth! He didn't give Vera a chance, and I shan't give him any. Damned if I will!'

He gave a start as the interphone buzzed. He picked up the instrument and Turner's voice came from the office below.

'He's coming, Sid. Be here in about ten minutes. I'll wait down here so I can let him in. Get the film ready.'

'It's done, sir. Let me know when he gets here.'

'I will.'

Sid put the instrument back on its rest and mooched about the box, hands in trouser pockets, brows down. All the bitter unhappiness, which he had felt at the death of Vera had returned to him. Whatever she had been he had loved her. Probably he was the only person who ever had — and she had been brutally murdered by a brilliant trick of ultrasonics.

'Right, Terry, you just wait! You just *wait* . . . ' Sid beat the wall gently with his massive fist; then very slowly he relaxed and covered his face with his hands. He sat down on the heavy bench and brooded until the interphone again buzzed. It was Turner.

'Cliff's got here now, Sid, and I've been explaining things to him. Naturally he'll co-operate. Start up the reel and join us in the Circle.'

'Okay, sir.'

Sid rang off, waited until he saw Turner and the service engineer come into the Circle, and then he started the machine and went out to join them. Cliff Dixon was a short, snub-nosed man with red hair. Superficially, he appeared to have no particular qualifications until one came to the subject of sound and sound projectors — then it would have been hard to find a man anywhere with such far reaching knowledge.

As Sid appeared Dixon merely looked

up once and nodded an acknowledgement; then he turned his attention back to the instrument he was adjusting. Sid recognized what it was. It had the appearance of a voltmeter with sensitive bright nodules projecting from its polished circular exterior.

'Frequency detector?' Sid questioned.

'Yes.' Cliff Dixon did not look up.

He finally got the instrument adjusted to his liking, then from the case he had brought with him he took out a series of short lengths of rod, rather like the canes of a sweep's brush but much smaller — and screwed one length into the other until he had a twenty foot extension with the detector screwed on to the topmost rod.

With the extension in his hand, the detector itself waving around the two houselights — one of the old type and one of the new — he began to walk about. In silence Sid and Turner watched him.

'I don't get the idea,' Turner said, puzzled. 'Sure he knows what he's doing, Sid?'

'There couldn't be anything surer than that, sir. The detector works like a stopwatch. It registers sound frequencies and the needle automatically stops at the highest recording it can make. They use those things in new cinemas for testing the vibration of sound in different parts of the building. If there is something supersonic that gadget will find it fast enough.'

Only when the film came to an end did Dixon stop his perambulations and lower his instrument carefully. When he had unscrewed it and studied it he gave a whistle.

'Hell's bells!' he exclaimed, startled. 'There is a frequency of ninety thousand vibrations a second registered here!'

'You mean — ultrasonic?' Sid demanded.

Cliff Dixon stared at him. 'Man alive, I'll say it is! The highest most human beings can hear is eighteen thousand vibrations a second, which is about the upper limit of a full symphony orchestra.'

'After which it becomes so high that it's inaudible and changes to pure vibration?' Turner asked earnestly.

'That's right,' the engineer agreed. 'Ninety thousand is definitely ultrasonic, but in these scientific days that isn't really very high. It may interest you to know that there are generators in use, specially made, which turn out an ultrasonic vibration of twelve million to the second. Used for testing flaws in steel and all that kind of thing. Just the same,' Dixon went on, thinking, 'this is definitely clever. Seems to bear out what you've been telling me, Mr. Turner.'

'Am I right in thinking that this ultrasonic vibration would not be affected by the rattle and clash of that sound track we heard just now?' Sid asked.

'Quite right. That makes no difference. Nothing can alter the fact that the film you ran emits ninety thousand vibrations a second. Noise has nothing to do with it . . . Let's take a look at that film. I'm fascinated.'

Sid nodded and led the way upstairs. In a few minutes he had stopped the racing projector and brought the film into the winding room. Dixon looked at it minutely in the bright light.

'This,' he said finally, 'if we forget everything else for the moment, is the work of a genius. You can see what's happened, can't you?'

'Matter of fact, no,' Sid growled. 'All I can see are a lot of small punctures which should produce a hum on the sound equipment.'

'Hum be damned — ' the engineer retorted. 'To create a *hum* those punctures would need to be more widely spaced. Actually they are so close that they're almost touching. They seem to have been deliberately made with some kind of fine-toothed wheel. The effect in the sound gate is for these dots to produce persistence of vibration –– an extremely high, thin note far above hearing range and in the ultrasonic scale. Result — ninety thousand vibrations a second. Finale — a falling globe from which the screws unravelled.'

Silence. Sid stood with his hands pushed deep in his trouser pockets, his eyes on the film. Turner wandered across to his jacket and pulled it on slowly.

'Are you going to call the police?'

317

Dixon asked. 'I'll tell them what I've told you if you like.'

'I prefer to think the business over first, Cliff,' Turner answered, catching a look from Sid. 'You've been a mighty big help to us, and I'm very much obliged.'

'You're welcome.' Dixon gave a shrug, then shook his head.

'I would never have thought such a thing of Terry. Only goes to show — you can't trust anybody. Well, that being all I'd better be on my way. I'll get my bag from the Circle.'

'I'll see you out and lock the doors,' Turner said, and followed behind the engineer as he left the winding room.

In five minutes Turner was back. He found Sid steadily winding up the film, his face grimly set.

'Well, Sid, what's next? Nothing for it but the police, is there? I think I ought to call them and let them see the evidence we've accumulated.'

'And suppose, legally, there isn't a way to prove that Terry is behind everything?' Sid questioned. 'I'm a projectionist, too, and I rethreaded the film which brought

318

down the globe. I might even get into a spot myself.'

'But that's ridiculous!' Turner protested.

Sid finished winding up the film and tucked the leader end into the spool. 'I'm a cautious bloke, sir. I'd feel a whole lot safer if Terry confessed, before witnesses. Then there wouldn't be any doubt as to the guilty party. The material evidence could be added afterwards.'

'Well, I — '

'A few hours can't make much difference now,' Sid insisted. 'I want to feel secure. The law's a funny thing.'

'How,' Turner asked, 'do you propose to make Terry confess?'

'There are ways and means. Criminals are always cowards at heart. I'll break him down, if you'll leave it to me to handle. I've a special stake in this, remember — Vera was the girl I loved, and the one I intended to marry.'

After a moment of thought Turner made up his mind.

'Very well, but you've got to act fast. Now all these facts are in hand I want action. The longer I delay the more the police will wonder why when they're called in.'

'I'll have action before the show ends tomorrow night,' Sid promised. 'Or rather tonight: I'd forgotten it's early morning.' He handed the reel of film over. 'You'd better take this, sir. It'll be wanted for examination by the police.'

Turner took it. 'I'll take it home with me. I don't trust that safe of mine anymore.'

'I'll start cleaning up,' Sid decided, going out of the winding room. 'There's glass and stuff to be cleared away and the houselights to be fixed up — old houselight to be taken down.'

12

Retribution

Terry arrived at the cinema the following morning with the conviction that there was something wrong somewhere. It was not that there was anything tangible to make him suspicious: it was an abstract thing, though how much of it was due to his own conscience and how much to the power of thought ranged against him he could not decide. He was brooding over it, ascending the stairs to the Circle, when a girl's voice gave him pause.

'And what's the matter with *you*, sourpuss?'

Terry came back to the world of reality. It was Kathleen Gatty who had spoken. She was sharp-nosed, keen eyed, and the kind of girl Terry did not particularly like.

'Nothing's the matter with me,' he retorted. 'Satisfied?'

'Just thought you looked as though you

321

needed a liver pill,' Kathleen said, getting busy again with her duster.

Terry weighed her up. She was attractive enough, in a way. He had lost two girls and had made up his mind that no girl is really worth bothering about — but primitive urge is not stifled that easily.

'What's the matter with you?' Kathleen asked, looking up in surprise. 'Am I coming apart somewhere, or what?'

'I was just thinking . . . We haven't seen much of each other in the time you've been here.'

'So what?'

Terry reflected, a memory crossing his mind. It would help to make conversation, anyway.

'I've been meaning to ask you, Kath. What did you mean by telling Sid that our hall speakers had resonance? A few days ago.'

'Someday I'll perhaps understand what you're talking about,' Kathleen responded. 'Matter of fact I hardly ever see Sid — more's the pity.'

Terry's expression changed. 'You mean

you *didn't* say anything to him about the speakers?'

'Why on earth should I? No business of mine, is it? I'm an usherette, not an operator . . . And as for us not seeing much of each other — you and I, I mean — I'm not shedding any tears.'

'Oh! You're not!'

'If I've any boy friend at all it's Sid.'

Terry hesitated, then without another word he turned and continued his journey up the stairs. He entered the winding room to find Billy leaning on the bench. The fact that Billy was thinking hard about something made him look vacant: to Terry it appeared just as though Billy were standing there waiting for him.

'What the hell's the matter with you?' Terry blazed at him. 'What's the idea of staring at me like that?'

'Eh?' Billy straightened up. 'Sorry, Terry, I was just thinking. What's the matter? Not feeling so good?'

Terry tugged off his jacket and hung it up. 'Women make me sick!' he declared. 'I never want to look at another woman as long as I live!'

'Get the brush off?' Billy asked; then without waiting for an answer he added, 'I know just how you feel. My girl friend's given me the air too. I wanted to kiss her last night and she socked me one! Now it's all over. I've decided to become a lifelong bachelor.'

Terry said nothing. He had not even heard. He was standing gazing morosely at the concrete floor, hands dug in his trousers pockets.

'Who walked out on you this time?' Billy inquired curiously. 'It couldn't have been Vera for obvious reasons.'

'Keep Vera's name out of it!' Terry snapped. 'Understand? Damn well shut up about Vera!'

'Okay,' Billy muttered, half frightened and half puzzled. 'No need to get sore at me.'

He turned his back and began to rewind the last reel from the performance the previous night. Terry watched him for a moment or two, then he went up the steps into the projection room. He expected to find Sid there, tidying up, but there was no sign of him. Even the fireproof shutters across the portholes had not been raised.

Scowling, Terry opened the spring door and shouted down:

'Hey! Where's Sid this morning?'

'Dunno, Terry. Ain't come yet. Mebbe he's scared that I'll beat him up when he comes. He gave me a trouncing yesterday.'

Terry let the spring door slam back into place. Unusual for Sid to be late. In fact he had never been behind time before. As for being ill, that was an impossible thought as far as the husky Sid was concerned. Terry looked at his watch. It was 9-30. So far, Sid was half an hour late.

'So Kath didn't mention anything about resonance, eh?' Terry muttered to himself, his face grim. 'Sid invented that as an excuse so he could go back stage. I just wonder *why* . . . '

He put up the fireproof shutters and opened the door that led on to the fire escape. The electric-lit gloom was lightened somewhat but not entirely dissipated by the slanting morning sunshine. The stray lingering odour of carbon fumes vanished before the fresh stirring of the air.

'Have to do his work for him, I suppose,' Terry told himself. 'Wonder what game he's got on?'

He turned to No. 2 machine and dusted it, then he looked inside the lamphouse. The carbons were in place in readiness for the matinee. It was a rule he insisted upon: the carboning-up should be done the night before to save time. With a small scoop and brush he cleaned out the carbon crumbs and then moved on to Machine No. 1, the projector he usually ran himself.

He still had that odd conviction that something was wrong somewhere. It was made all the more potent by the fact that Sid was not here to time. Where *was* the man? What was he up to? Why hadn't he come —

Terry's thoughts came to a dead stop. He had raised the heavy asbestos-lined side of the lamphouse of his machine to clean out the bits as he had with the twin projector. He stared at the carbons. Contrary to his ruling, no carboning-up had been done. The positive and negative jaws were tight together with two burned-out stubs of electrode half an inch apart.

'Some use giving orders,' he sighed, then he strode to the swing door, dragged it open, and bawled for Billy. That youth, already somewhat jittery, came hurrying to obey.

'What's the use of my giving orders if you're going to ignore them?' Terry demanded. 'Look at that arc!'

Billy looked. Terry came over to him.

'I've told you time and again, Billy, that you should carbon-up the night before. You've done the other machine, but not this one. Sliding out of your work because it happened to be my day off yesterday, eh?'

'Course I didn't.' Billy defiantly pushed out his lips. 'I carboned-up this arc last night when the show was over, same as I always do. I put two new carbons in, too!'

'Looks like it, doesn't it?' Terry asked sourly. 'Burned down to the limit, just as they must have been when the show finished last night.'

'Honest, Terry, I *did* carbon-up.'

Terry looked at the youth intently, a frown gathering.

'That's the honest truth, Billy?'

'Cross my heart! I've never forgotten yet. I do my job properly, and you know it.' Billy looked again at the carbons and then scratched his head. 'I just don't understand this one bit. It looks as though the arc has been used since I left it last night — but I don't see how that could be. Sid isn't here, so he couldn't have the machine this morning for anything — and I'm darned sure I haven't. What'll I do? Re-carbon it?'

'Never mind. I'll do it. Get back to your winding.'

'I'll do it if you like. It's my job.'

'Get back to your winding!' Terry shouted.

Billy stared and then went. He was a deeply puzzled youth by the time he got back to the winding room. He did not even whistle.

In the projection room, Terry remained quite still for several moments, staring at the carbon stubs; then he fitted new carbons and swept up the bits. He threw the stubs in the waste bin and stood pondering. He had no doubts whatever that Billy had spoken the truth. There was no reason why he should not have carboned-up as usual, for he was an industrious worker and loved his job.

Yes, he had spoken the truth — but the machine had been used afterwards, and nobody but Sid could be responsible for that.

Why had it been used?

Terry looked up sharply at the sound of heavy feet coming up the iron steps of the fire escape. With an effort he tried to cast the look of bitter suspicion from his face. A shadow fell across the polished stone floor of the projection room and Sid's big, ungainly figure came into view. He was in old flannel trousers and an open-necked shirt, his sandy hair sprouting untidily as usual. He was not even shaved.

'All right, slang me,' he invited, seeing Terry looking at him. 'For some reason or other I overslept. Can't remember when I did that. Sorry. I'll soon catch up.'

'There's nothing on which to catch up. I've done your work for you, including the arcs.'

Sid shrugged. 'Okay — thanks. Then I'd better get down to the winding room and see about spooling up the programme for tomorrow morning's rehearsal.'

Terry stared at him. The remark about the arcs had evidently not made the least impression. In truth it had not. The fact that he had left the burned-down stubs of carbon in the jaws had not even occurred to Sid. It being out of his usual routine he had never given it a thought.

Leaving the projection room he went down below to commence his ordinary work. Terry reflected for a while, then he too went below. He glanced in the winding room — saw Sid and Billy both at their jobs and slanging each other — then he continued his journey into the Circle.

The doorman was there, examining seats, and so were two of the cleaning women with their buckets and mops. Terry nodded to them but said nothing. With apparent casualness he went to the back of the Circle and sat down. From here he could not be seen from the portholes of the projection room, being below the line of vision.

Taking out a cigarette he lighted it and then gazed around him. For some reason a show had been run after the normal performance on the previous night — or at any rate a film had. His only hope lay in finding a clue somewhere as to what had been happening.

The florid face of one of the cleaning women looked across at him.

'Wish I 'ad your job, Terry m'lad! Nothin' to do but sit on your backside and smoke! Money for old rope. What are you supposed to be doin'? Waitin' for a rehearsal?'

'Get on with your job, Clara, and I'll get on with mine,' Terry answered shortly.

''Ark at 'im!' exclaimed the doorman, staring. 'Gettin' real 'igh brow, ain't he?'

Terry gave a glance of contempt and then resumed his seemingly idle survey of the Circle. He looked up at the new houselights.

Nothing wrong there: they were just as

331

they had been — the vellum shades and the 300-watt lamps, screwed into the sockets. He lowered his gaze to the floor. He dared not look too closely for fear of attracting attention. As far as he could tell there was nothing lying about which might help him to understand why Machine No. 1 had been run after the performance.

If it *had* been run. His mind strayed for a moment to Mark Turner; then he remembered that the boss hardly knew the difference between a spool and a lens. No, if anybody had run that machine it had been Sid . . . Sid.

Troubled by his inability to discover anything to confirm his suspicions, Terry got to his feet at last and stood thinking what he could do next. He raised his eyes as Kathleen Gatty came into the Circle and looked about her.

'Anybody here seen Harry?' she called.

''ere,' the doorman growled, rising from behind a seat. 'What d'you want, lass?'

'I've two buckets of rubbish to empty — cigarette ends, ice cream cartons, papers, and such. I want to know which dustbin they go in. I'm new to this part of my job, remember. There are two bins outside — one with glass in and one with clinkers. Which is it?'

'Not the one with the clinkers in: that's the cellar bin. And don't keep bothering me. I'm busy.'

Kathleen went off actively and Terry frowned. *Glass?* He knew which two bins had been referred to, and Kathleen was not the first usherette transferred to new cleaning duties who had asked which bin to use. Glass? Queer for there to be glass. Lemonade had not been served recently: only ice cream cartons.

Terry left the Circle and strolled downstairs. He went into the stalls, apparently on a technical mission, and spent some time examining the extinguished safety lights on the side walls as though to be certain they were in order. He waited until Kathleen came in again from the yard at the back of the cinema. When he was satisfied that she was once more at work cleaning the foyer he slid out by an emergency door and hurried over to the waste bins.

He ignored the bin containing clinkers and lifted the lid off its neighbour. He gazed down on a mass of glass fragments, most of them thin and curved. He picked up a piece and examined it.

It was not tumbler glass: it was much too fine.

With an increasing urgency he raked amongst the debris with the end of a pencil and then selected one large javelin with a distinct bow shape. He read the clearly visible wording on the glass —

200 Volt. 300-watt. Triple Coiled

'From a houselight bulb,' he breathed, staring in front of him and letting the glass drop from his fingers. 'One of the new bulbs we put up recently. And all this glass too! Must have been more than one bulb gone west.'

Instinctively he snatched at the implications. His machine had been run after the performance. Sid had arrived late due to oversleeping, evidently because he had worked on into the night — and now these shattered remains of bulbs! With savage urgency Terry searched further, and before long, lower down in the general rubbish of cartons and papers, he came to the remains of the bulbs themselves — two of them, their filaments twisted and broken but the brass screwcaps still new.

'He *knows* . . . ' Terry put the lid slowly back on the dustbin. 'If he does he can't have told anybody else yet or I'd probably have been arrested by this time. He must have got hold of the film somehow, or duplicated the effect, and proved for himself what I did. If I run for it I'll stand convicted. On the other hand, if I can find a way to take care of him before he starts to shoot off his big mouth . . . '

He re-entered the cinema slowly, musing. Sid was a grim danger. He had always been the trouble spot. Perhaps he had a lot more investigating to do before he accumulated the final evidence. Before that happened he had got to be taken care of . . . completely.

Terry returned upstairs and glanced in the winding room. Sid and Billy were both busy preparing the programme for the following day . . . With apparent unconcern Terry took the film book from the shelf, made his usual entries, and then lounged up to the projection room.

There ought to be some way to deal with Sid. Some kind of accident, electrical perhaps. He no longer cared if it meant another murder. If he did not act quickly he was finished.

Electrical? Hardly. Sid was an expert and he would not be likely to fall for any electrical trick that might wipe him out. He was always wary.

'Must be some way,' Terry insisted to himself.

He wandered out on to the fire escape and stood gazing over the yards below. The morning sunlight was brilliant, the wind fresh. He walked down the .four steps to the main grid where the fire escape took a sharp turn. He stood pondering.

'Don't do much work, do you?' called a voice from below.

He glanced down. Kathleen Gatty was down there, foreshortened by the hundred-and-fifty-foot drop. She was busily cleaning the brass bars of the side emergency door.

Terry did not answer her. His expression changed slowly and a gleam came into his eyes.

'It's a chance,' he whispered finally. 'We never use this escape after dark. People might suspect, but they'd never be able to prove. If it doesn't kill him it'll lay him out and anything he says won't be worth considering as evidence . . . '

★   ★   ★

Throughout the remainder of the morning, and all through the afternoon, there was nothing in Sid's manner to suggest that he was waiting for a moment to strike. He talked and grinned and ragged young Billy. He behaved indeed in such a normal way that once or twice Terry found himself wondering if he had not been wrong in his judgment, if there were not some other explanation for the burned carbons and broken glass.

'Stop lulling yourself into false security,' he told himself, when the matinee was over. 'Act first — and be sure!'

After tea, Sid was back first, and Billy a

moment or two after him. The youth had the expression of one forced to work with lunatics.

'Y'know something?' he asked, hanging up his jacket.

'What?' Sid rolled up his shirtsleeves to display powerful forearms.

'I think Terry's going off it!'

Sid grinned. 'Taken you a long time to arrive at that conclusion, hasn't it?'

'Honest, apeman, I'm not kidding. He's behaved more queerly today than at any time before. Wonder if the work's getting on his nerves, or something? For instance — this morning he played heck with me for not carboning up No. 1 machine last night when we'd finished, and I know I *did*! I'm darned sure you don't love this place so much that you'd come back after hours and try out a show, so the only thing I can think of is that he put two old bits of carbon in the arc for himself so as to find an excuse to play old Harry with me.'

Sid compressed his lips and swore softly to himself. Then he asked, 'What did he do finally?'

'Nothing. I thought he was going to flay me alive. Instead he told me to get back to my work and that he'd carbon up for himself. That was crazy enough, but this afternoon he came down here when you were running your machine and landed a real beauty.'

Sid stared fixedly at the winding bench. So Terry had found out that the carbons had been used. He must *know*, or at least have formed an assumption —

'Do you want to listen or not?' Billy demanded, and Sid gave a start.

'Huh? Oh, sorry, kid . . . You were saying?'

'He gave me strict orders to lock this outer winding room door the moment it gets dark tonight — in case of burglars. I'm not to go outside on any account, and when I leave it's to be by the front door. Can't think why he needs to tell me that since it's too dangerous to use the fire escape after dark in any case. I tell you straight — he's barmy!'

Sid gave a shrug. He was hardly interested in the youth's vapourings. He took the first reel out of the bin and went up to the projection room to lace up.

'Better be on my guard,' he told himself. 'He may try and pull something, and one more murder won't make any difference since he's already a killer. I don't doubt for a minute that he'd try to dispose of me if he has any suspicions . . . '

He assumed a casual air ten minutes later when Terry came to do his share of the work, but throughout the evening he and Sid hardly spoke to each other.

Outside, the late summer night began to draw in, even earlier than usual with the approach of rainclouds. In the intervals when he was not at his machine Terry lounged out on to the fire escape and smoked. The last reel of the feature picture was on Sid's machine, which left Terry to lounge about as he chose. He spent a while outside and Sid assumed he was having a smoke — then he came back into the box again.

It was night outside now, with wet, rising wind. Sid looked at his reel in the top spool box. Three quarters of it to go yet.

'Sid!'

Sid gave a start and looked round the end of the projector's lamphouse. Terry was standing in the black oblong of open doorway, staring into the night.

'You say something?' Sid asked.

'Yes.' Terry turned and came back into the bright light. 'Somebody is in the entry outside, calling you. Sounds like a girl's voice.'

'Calling *me*?' Sid looked mystified. 'Can't be!'

'It sound to me like Kath Gatty. You're a bit thick with her these days, aren't you?'

'Well, I dunno about that . . . ' Sid frowned and rubbed the back of his neck.

'You'd better look,' Terry said. 'Perhaps it's her early night and she's got a message for you. Go on — I'll take over your machine.'

Sid shrugged and walked across to the doorway. He gripped the fire-escape rail and stared into the dark.

'Ahoy there! Somebody call?'

There was no answer. He half turned to descend the fire escape and shout again. Might be an answer from the lower position where his voice would carry better — then suddenly he caught a glimpse of Terry's face as he stood in the projection room. He was not watching the running machine, nor was he looking through the porthole. He was gazing towards the projection room's open outer door with a malignant, homicidal stare. It was so malevolent that it checked Sid in mid-action . . . A premonition of danger crossed his mind, and passed.

Slowly he came back into the projection room and Terry's strange look relaxed. He appeared ghastly pale and his face glistened in the reflected blue-white glare of the arclight.

'Nobody there,' Sid said simply. 'You're imagining things.'

Terry shrugged. 'I could have sworn . . . I must have been mistaken.'

Sid opened the top spool box of his machine. There was ten minutes running time left. He nodded to himself, passed close beside the amplifier rack, and then looked at Terry intently.

Terry looked back, a startled light kindling in his eyes. He had never seen

Sid's face quite so mercilessly hard before.

'Anything the matter?' Terry burst out abruptly.

'Talking of mistakes,' Sid answered deliberately, 'you made quite a few, didn't you? When you murdered Vera with that falling houselight trick?'

Terry, leaning against the wall, straightened up. The moment he had so long feared had come. Sid had worked out the business to the last detail and was ready for action. And what defence was there against him?

'Vera? Murdered her?' Terry stumbled over his own words. 'I never did anything of the sort!'

'I know differently. The only thing to make it conclusive is your own admission of the fact. That I mean to get.'

'Don't be a damned idiot!' Terry snapped. 'And have you forgotten that we're running a show? Look to your machine — '

'The machine's all right.' Sid was dead calm. 'The automatic feed's on and there are ten minutes to run. In that ten

343

minutes we're going to be busy . . . ' He swung, slammed the bolt across the spring door. Billy, therefore, could not now enter.

Terry looked about him desperately.

'Well?' Sid asked deliberately. 'Do I get the truth?'

'What's the *matter* with you?' Terry yelled. 'Even if I had anything to confess to — which I haven't — it wouldn't do you any good without witnesses! But you're too blasted dumb to realize that, I suppose?'

Sid reached out his hand to the interphone as it buzzed sharply. He snapped over the switch that stopped the buzzing.

'That — that may be the boss!' Terry gasped, beginning to sweat. 'I'd better answer it — '

'You'll answer me! Never mind the boss!'

'But — ' Terry's words were hurled down his throat as Sid's right fist lashed up and slammed into his face. With dizzying impact Terry struck the wall and half fell down beside it. Sid yanked him up, hit him again, and yet again, finally sending him stumbling into the corner between the wall and the closed spring door.

Terry crouched, watching his chance, his lip bleeding. His eyes followed the movement of Sid's right hand. Sid snatched the pliers from the rack and then pulled open the door of the arc lamphouse. The blinding white light fell on Terry and he jerked his eyes away. Grim-faced, Sid switched off the arc and then turned the houselight dimmer up slightly so the audience outside was not in total darkness.

The machine ran on, the monitor-speaker chattering.

'What are you *doing*?' Terry screamed. 'You're killing the show, you madman!'

He stopped, staring in horror. With the pliers Sid snapped off the red-hot positive carbon and swung it round. With his massive right arm he crushed Terry into the corner. With his left hand he lowered the glowing carbon towards him.

'You'd better speak up!' Sid breathed, fury making his voice hardly audible. 'So help me, I'll burn every inch of hide off your rotten bones if you don't — '

'I didn't do anything!' Terry screamed, and his scream broke in a shriek as the point of the searing carbon bit into his cheek.

'*Out with it!*' Sid bellowed, and jabbed the carbon again — this time on Terry's neck.

The pain was too much — Sid's strength too great. Terry writhed and squirmed desperately.

'Not again!' he shouted desperately. 'All right, I did it! I made the houselight come down — '

'With a Travelogue film and vibration?'

'Yes! Anyway, she deserved to die! She was rotten! She stole my money — '

Sid flung the pliers away from him. The carbon clinked on the stone floor.

'So that was how you got your wallet back?' he demanded. 'And she caught you thieving, didn't she? *Didn't* she?'

'Yes. I was — '

A blow in the jaw hurled Terry across the projection room to the outer door. Sid hurried forward, his fists bunched, ready to follow up his advantage. He ignored a violent pounding on the spring door.

Terry staggered up, dishevelled, blood streaming from his cut mouth.

'What more do you want?' he shouted. 'Leave me alone! We can't argue out here — Not out here! *Sid* — '

With the impact of a pile-driver Sid's fist slammed up again. Terry spun round, clutched the fire escape rail dizzily, and then slipped backwards down the rain-greased steps. He gave a wild cry that abruptly stopped and then ended in a thud. Puzzled, Sid blundered down the iron four steps to drag Terry back —

Abruptly the world vanished and Sid found himself swinging with one hand to an iron step, drizzle soaking into his face. Savagely he fought his way back, the horrifying truth biting into his mind. The two plates which formed the floor of the escape turning had been raised edgewise against the rail so there was no longer any floor! Then, somewhere down there . . .

'The devil!' Sid breathed, rubbing his grazed arms. 'So *that* was why he said somebody was calling me. He thought I'd blunder down here and drop. And I would have too — but for that look on his face which stopped me. No wonder he didn't want to fight out here! No wonder he told Billy to keep inside after dark . . . '

He seized the plates and lowered them back into place. He had just finished the task when the outer door of the winding room flew open. Light gushed into the night. Turner, Billy, and the doorman came into view.

Turner clattered up the steps and gripped Sid's arm.

'Sid, are you all right? We couldn't get in by the inner door of the box.'

'I'm all right,' Sid acknowledged. 'Terry's down there in the entry somewhere. He — he made a dash for it, and jumped.'

'Get down there, Harry — and quick!' Turner snapped to the doorman — and the doorman went, his torch waving.

'Who did what?' Billy asked incredulously.

'Shut up, kid,' Sid retorted. 'Get back to the winding room. You'll know everything before long.'

Puzzled, Billy obeyed. Sid mounted the

348

steps back to the projection room, went over to the amplifier bank and cut off the sound; then he turned to Turner.

'What did you do?' Turner demanded. 'Suddenly the sound went off and instead everybody heard you and Terry arguing — and then came his confession. What happened?'

'We needed witnesses,' Sid said doggedly. 'And we got 'em! Everybody in the theatre heard that confession. Without Terry noticing, I switched the button on the amplifier bank. It cut out the sound on the film and instead livened the mike. I did it deliberately. Terry didn't know. The film sound was running, on the monitor as usual, and you can't hear the hall speakers in here. When I cut off the projector arc I put up the houselights so as to prevent any panic in the audience.'

'Well, you couldn't have been more thorough. I couldn't understand the set-up, and that was why I buzzed you . . . And you say Terry jumped for it?'

Sid gave a slow nod, then he and Turner glanced round as the doorman came in by the emergency doorway. His plum coloured uniform was soiled and muddy.

'I want an 'and to get the body out of sight, sir,' he said, looking at Turner. 'Before the audience comes out and finds it. It might happen at any moment if any of them girls open the side exits.'

Sid swung to the microphone and switched it on again.

'Keep your seats, ladies and gentle-men,' he intoned. 'There has been a slight mix-up in the sound. We'll run the last reel again and at the close of the performance the manager will explain from the stage. Thank you.'

Sid switched off, pulled the film free of the projector, and then began to spin it back to the start.

'I'll give you a hand, Harry,' Turner said, looking at the doorman. 'You said — the *body*?'

'Yes, sir. 'E's dead, sir.' The doorman licked his dry lips. 'Looks to me like a broken neck . . . '

Turner met Sid's eyes. Then Sid snapped the gate of the projector and began to rearrange the arc carbons.

Without another word Turner left the projection room and Sid could hear his feet and the doorman's receding into distance down the steps of the fire escape.

There was a pause. The film started up again and Sid put out the houselights. Then Billy was hammering on the spring door. He looked pale and scared as Sid opened it.

'What happened?' he asked huskily. 'Something — to Terry?'

'Yes.' Sid was coldly deliberate. 'He fell off the fire escape. Greasy steps in the rain. He always knew a thing like that might happen, which was why he warned you to keep off the escape after darkness.'

'You — you mean he's dead?' Billy's eyes were round.

'Yes, kid — he's dead. Looks like you'll have me for a chief from now on . . . Now get back to your work. The show's got to go on, remember.'

The spring door closed again. Sid inspected his machine and then looked towards the long oblong of outer doorway, through which the rain was drifting . . .

CLIMATE INCORPORATED
THE FIVE MATCHBOXES
EXCEPT FOR ONE THING
BLACK MARIA, M.A.
ONE STEP TOO FAR
THE THIRTY-FIRST OF JUNE
THE FROZEN LIMIT
ONE REMAINED SEATED
THE MURDERED SCHOOLGIRL
SECRET OF THE RING
OTHER EYES WATCHING
I SPY . . .
FOOL'S PARADISE
DON'T TOUCH ME
THE FOURTH DOOR
THE SPIKED BOY
THE SLITHERERS
MAN OF TWO WORLDS
THE ATLANTIC TUNNEL
THE EMPTY COFFINS
LIQUID DEATH